For Mom, Dad, and Carolyne

"The silence of an African jungle on a dark night needs to be experienced to be realized; it is most impressive, especially when one is absolutely alone and isolated from one's fellow creatures, as I was then."

John Henry Patterson
The Man-Eaters of Tsavo (1907)

PROLOGUE

The morning sun glinted down on the hood of the Jeep as it climbed higher into the sky above the Serengeti. Sitting in the passenger seat, Solomon Akeda squinted and retrieved a pair of sunglasses dangling from his shirt collar. The grassland sprawled out in all directions as far as the eye could see, occasionally dotted by a small cluster of acacia trees. It was a breathtaking sight, but one that he was accustomed to.

"How far?" he asked the driver.

"Five minutes, tops," the park ranger said, wiping sweat from his brow. He looked nervous.

Akeda bit his lip and glanced back out at the plains, hoping to see some of the animals. This whole thing had him on edge. The warden had requested him specifically, but Akeda had no clue why they needed a zoologist. The park staff dealt with animal problems all the time; he was simply there to study them.

Born in Johannesburg, Solomon Akeda had always been fascinated with African wildlife. This obsession carried him through undergrad at the University of Cape Town, widely considered to be the best on the continent, and later into field research for the same institution. His focus was now ethology, which examined the correlation between zoological behaviors and conditions in nature. He was up here in Tanzania to study social transmission in hyenas and hadn't been planning on heading out into the park until the afternoon. That changed when a vehicle with the Serengeti National Park logo on the side pulled into his team's camp just before seven in the morning.

Akeda had been asleep in his tent when his assistant Bekker woke him and told him there was a ranger here to see him. At first he thought that idiot Kruger back at Cape Town had mucked up the permits again, but instead he saw the man who now sat beside him, looking frightened and asking him to please come with him.

"What's going on?" Akeda had asked.

"We need you to look at something. It's urgent."

"Can you tell me what it is?"

The ranger had shaken his head. "I can't explain. It is best to see it."

Then they were off. That had been over twenty minutes ago. The ranger had been tight-lipped ever since and didn't even play any music; there was just the sound of the wind whipping past the open windows and wheels rolling over the uneven terrain. Akeda almost dozed off – he had been planning on getting another hour or so of sleep – but then the Jeep hit a bump and he jolted back into consciousness.

Up ahead he could see three other park vehicles stopped thirty feet from a lone acacia. Akeda could see several other rangers milling around a short distance beyond. Though they were spread out, they all appeared to be looking at something on the ground. The Jeep came to a halt and Akeda climbed out. A heavyset man was supervising the rangers, standing with his back turned to them. At the sound of car doors closing, the man turned around and started towards them.

"You must be Solomon Akeda," the man said, looking relieved. He extended his hand. "Matthew Diawara, Chief Warden."

Akeda shook it. "What's the issue?"

Diawara began leading him past the other Jeeps. "See for yourself."

A few feet later, he froze. A chill shot down his spine as he took it all in. "Jesus Christ," was all he could manage.

Before him, spread out within a fifty-foot radius, were the carcasses of at least twenty zebras. Each of them was covered with horrific gashes. Huge, bloody chunks had been ripped from their necks but the damage done to the rest of the bodies was inconsistent. Some had been disemboweled with their entrails strewn about, but others had only been partially eaten. Akeda saw some with minimal wounds aside from the throat gashes, as if whatever had done this had killed them all quickly and only consumed what it needed before moving on.

He stepped forward and crouched to examine one of the more heavily mutilated carcasses. The zebra's head remained barely attached, tethered to the rest of its body by a few ragged strands of flesh and a bent spinal cord. The animal's viscera lay in a gory tangle spread out several feet from its open abdomen. Blood had seeped into the soil and stained the nearby blades of grass.

The violence of the scene wasn't what bothered him; Akeda had been well aware of the "red tooth and claw" nature of the biological world ever since he started watching National Geographic documentaries as a kid. No, it was that in all his years of studying animals he had *never* seen anything like what lay before him, let alone heard of it.

"Do you know what could have done this?" Diawara asked from behind him.

Without turning around, Akeda shook his head. His eyes scanned the carnage laid out before him, moving from carcass to carcass, turning the possibilities over in his mind. Then he spotted something on the ground a few feet away and got up for a closer inspection.

Emerging from the zone of the kill was a pair of four-toed bloody imprints on the turf. Leaning down, he could see they were roughly five inches across. Normally, he would've immediately said they belonged to a lion. But given the circumstances, he wasn't sure. Lions certainly didn't behave this way, not any lions that he had ever heard of.

The trail of prints continued forward, becoming less bloody with each step the creature had taken. Akeda suddenly saw several more tracks nearby, leading away from the other carcasses. He walked over to inspect them, the sun beating down on the back of his neck as the day grew warmer. He wished he'd brought a hat. At first it was confusing to follow them because they crossed each other multiple times, but Akeda counted at least five separate tracks made by the same type of animal.

A pack.

His gaze followed the trails as they became a formation and slipped off into the expansive savanna beyond. Slowly he turned around to see the others staring at him, waiting to hear his thoughts on the matter.

Akeda opened his mouth, then stopped, realizing he was speechless.

PART I

PREDATORS

MUSEUM

The first lioness was clambering onto the buffalo's back, her open jaws descending towards the creature's hide for the first bite. The second was turning to dodge the falling animal, which had a vaguely terrified expression cemented on its face as it began to topple. It was a snapshot of a life and death struggle, frozen in time.

Of course, Sydney knew that just like every other exhibit in this room, it had been purposely staged. These three animals had probably never even come into contact in real life, yet here they were: immortalized together as an example of nature's breathtaking savagery. They had been just like that every time she visited this place since she was a little kid.

The Smithsonian National Museum of Natural History was situated halfway on the Mall between the Capitol Building and the Washington Monument. Growing up in Potomac, Maryland, coming here with her family had been one of her favorite childhood weekend excursions. They had called it "Stones and Bones" for the geology exhibition and the fossil collection, but the Hall of Mammals had always held a special place in her heart.

Even at age twenty-one, Sydney Marlowe still felt the same childish tingle of excitement walking into the open area of the African Mammals portion of the exhibit. Beneath a high glass ceiling, taxidermied animals were displayed in small slivers of their former lives. An impala stood on a rocky outcropping, a giraffe stretched its neck to reach the dangling leaves of a tree branch, zebras drank from a riverbank, and a magnificent lion roared on a podium while the information board beneath it read "Africa" and provided information on the climate of the grasslands. The far wall was painted to look like the savanna woodlands but all the other sides of the exhibit were white save for some stylistic milky-white glass panes along the walls. Lighting was rigged above and below certain displays to highlight them for dramatic effect when it became dark.

What impressed Sydney the most was that each individual exhibit was quite minimalist in style, yet still managed to convey a larger world beyond what it depicted. She preferred it to the zoo because the staging allowed for a more theatrical feel than watching sun-baked lions lounge in the shade on a hot July day. Also, the museum was air conditioned.

A tall, black man who was the same age as her brushed past, taking it all in.

"So…what do you think?" she asked.

"Impressive," he said with a British accent, turning to look at the two lionesses killing the buffalo off to the left. "Can't believe in three years I've never come here." Born in London, Andy Baker had spent most of his life there until he came to

Georgetown.

"You need to get out more," she teased.

He glanced back at her and smirked. "You're one to talk. I'm the one always dragging your sorry behind everywhere."

She laughed and scratched her arm awkwardly, knowing he was right. Andy had come to the States without knowing a soul and yet, by the end of the first semester he had become one of the most popular people in their year. He seemingly attracted only positive attention, and making friends came naturally to him. Sydney, however, felt she was a few steps behind in that regard. Sometimes she wondered if Andy only hung out with people like her as friendship charity cases, but his care always seemed genuine. Besides, they had had innumerable heart-to-heart discussions over the past few years. She shook off the thought as he walked up the ramp towards the center of the room and started to follow him.

Andy stopped in front of the artificial riverbank display, looking closely at the figure of a giraffe splaying its legs to bring its long neck down to drink. A hippo stood beside it, looking off in a different direction with its enormous jaws agape. A few shrubs were placed around the animals but the ground was marble like a countertop rather than the color of dirt. Even though she knew she'd never get so close to such fauna in real life, she'd always had a fantasy of visiting Africa and going on a safari along the Serengeti plains to see something that wasn't just a recreation.

And in two days, her dream would come true.

She stepped closer. "I can't wait."

"Me neither," he said, looking at the zebras now. "You finished packing?"

She chuckled. "Haven't started. My mom's gonna kill me."

"I suppose we're lucky. Not many biotech firms that I've heard of have their own game reserve."

"But it belongs to Sans, right?" she said.

"It was his family's originally, but he's repurposed it for the company." Andy turned away from the display to look at her. "He seems a bit off, if you ask me."

"For multi-millionaires, I believe the term is *eccentric*."

"*Enigmatic* would better suit him. From what my dad tells me, he hasn't left the reserve in about three years. Some say he's gone off his trolley."

Sydney shrugged. "Maybe he just doesn't like to deal with people that much. So what?" *I can hardly blame him*, she thought.

"Being a recluse doesn't really mix with running a corporation. From what I hear, his introversion is starting to get on the board's nerves."

"Not all introverts are recluses."

"That's not what I meant, Sydney."

"You haven't even met this guy yet. Without him, the company wouldn't be a leader in its field. He obviously knows what he's doing."

"I'm not doubting the company, I'm doubting *him*. I mean, grad schools are going to shit bricks when they see 'SansCorp Field Researcher, Tanzania' on our resumes," Andy said. "But don't you think there's something slightly odd about someone who has been away from civilization for all that time by choice? Especially when they show no signs of going back anytime soon?"

"I *guess*…" Sydney figured if she had a private game reserve and could run a billion-dollar company without ever leaving its confines, she'd probably stay there as long as she could.

SansCorp was a major bioengineering firm, up there with Gilead, Amgen, Celgene, and Regeneron. Headquartered in Bethesda, Maryland, it specialized in everything from growing artificial organs to gene therapy techniques and cloning technologies. The CEO, William Sans, was born in Geneva to a

British mother and a Swiss father, who founded the company in 1986. Sans was raised in Switzerland before attending Harvard and Stanford. Beyond that, everyone only knew one thing about him: he loved hunting. The only photo she had ever seen of him smiling had him crouched beside an enormous lion with a hunting rifle in his hand, wearing khaki shorts and safari attire. All the other pictures online were of him looking stern in various suits. He didn't seem like one to give off a warm vibe.

For the first time ever, four interns had been selected to become field researchers at the reserve this summer. Over the next two weeks they would serve as assistants at the company's facilities there, where Sans oversaw the implementation of their latest technologies. He himself had selected the four based on applications open only to this year's interns.

This Tanzania gig was a golden opportunity. She'd wanted to be a doctor her whole life, but getting into medical school these days was so competitive it practically required applicants to have discovered a cure for cancer. If you were anything less than perfect, they ignored you, and this position was her ace in the hole. Plenty of prospective graduate students had internships, but few had anything this high-level. Her supervisor would be none other than the CEO of a company that ranked fifth in possession of its industry's market share.

At that point, the fact that she was getting an all-inclusive trip to Africa seemed like icing on the cake, as it had been such a longtime desire of hers.

The truth was, she was unimaginably excited.

She turned around and looked at the display directly across from her. A leopard was perched up in a tree, the carcass of an impala draped over a branch. The predator appeared perfectly relaxed as it stared off into the distance, knowing its meal was secure from the prowling hyena on the ground below. Though the tree was located in the middle of the hall, Sydney could still picture it being surrounded by a grand savanna, the leopard gazing at the sunset as the horizon turned orange on the brink of dark. Its only concern was survival. Its only guiding logic was primal instinct. Nothing more and certainly nothing less.

She sighed, feeling almost envious of such a lifestyle.

SIMBA KISHINDO

The Cessna 208 Grand Caravan banked right in a wide arc and when it leveled again, Sydney groggily peered out the window on her left to see the vastness of the plains. The prairie grass all blurred together to look like a sea of faded green, trees were reduced to tiny specks, and the occasional river wound through the landscape like a snake. It seemed to go on forever.

She'd seen many pictures of the Serengeti before, but none taken from the air. And besides, this was better than staring at something on Google Images. She was actually here. It had taken them nearly twenty hours to get to Kenya. There were no direct flights from Washington, D.C. so they had flown from Dulles to Zurich and Zurich to Nairobi with a three-hour layover in-between. Sydney had tried to get some rest during the first leg but she'd always had a terrible time sleeping on planes. She'd managed to snooze on the second flight out of sheer exhaustion, but even then jet lag had cut into her initial excitement of landing in Africa. It had taken a moment for it to sink in that she was halfway around the world from home, in a land she'd only seen in picture books and Disney films.

For the past two hours or so, they had been on Sans's private plane that brought in supplies weekly and, on rare occasions, visitors. She glanced around the cabin. It was neatly furnished with plush white leather seats and polished wood paneling. It could fit eight passengers, four on each side of a small aisle, and each side had two chairs facing opposite across a table that folded out of the wall.

Across from her was Andy, who was reading a copy of the Smithsonian magazine he had picked up at the museum a few days ago. To the right of her were the two other interns: Brandon Conway, an athletic redhead from Louisiana, and Courtney Akita, a petite-looking girl from Vancouver. She had first met them at the SansCorp offices toward the end of May, but Sydney had never really spoken with them much. She knew Brandon studied at Dartmouth and Courtney went to McGill, but other than that she couldn't say much about them.

They had been chatting with each other fairly amicably for most of the trip and she hadn't wanted to cut in or intrude. In retrospect, she supposed she'd had an opportunity when Andy started talking to them – Andy could strike up a conversation with anyone – but she didn't want to look like an idiot when she had to continue the talk forward. It was so much easier with friends she knew. People always judge you more the first few times they interact with you.

"How's everyone feeling?" came a voice from behind her. She turned to see a slim, middle-aged Asian woman standing in the aisle, her hands gripping the backs of Sydney's and Brandon's chairs in the event of sudden turbulence. She was Ellie Chang, the

CFO of SansCorp. Behind where she stood, Sydney saw the other executive chaperone for the trip: a trim, goateed balding man who had introduced himself as Richard Jones. He hadn't said anything else since and was currently looking out his window with an empty expression.

"Tired," Courtney said, yawning and scratching her short black hair. "How much longer?"

Chang glanced at her watch. "About half an hour more. Almost there." She flashed a smile, trying to be cordial. She sat down on the seat behind Sydney, moving up the arm rest so she could keep her legs in the aisle and have a direct line of sight to the rest of them. "I know what you're studying from your files, but what about your career plans?"

Sydney nearly sighed. At her energy level, the last thing she wanted to do was talk about her future with a bunch of strangers. Chang was clearly trying to make small talk – just trying to be nice. Sometimes she hated when people did that.

"Computational neuroscience researcher. Oddly specific, I know," Brandon said with a smile. He had a charming Southern drawl.

"Not at all," Chang said. "When I was seven, I told my family I wanted to be a pediatric anesthesiologist."

"I'm going to work in the pharmaceutical industry," Courtney piped up with a matter-of-fact tone that made Sydney want to roll her eyes.

Chang simply nodded and looked to Andy. "I'm aiming for medical school. After that, I'm not sure yet."

"That's perfectly respectable," she said, now turning her gaze to Sydney.

She felt her shoulders tense up and a knot formed in the pit of her stomach. "Um…medical…school," she managed, her eyes darting around and looking anywhere but Chang's general direction. The CFO simply nodded.

Courtney saw her opening. "For grad school, I want to go to Columbia for a dual MD/MBA degree."

"Funny, that's what Billy Sans did at Stanford. I was only in the MBA program and given the workload of that alone, I thought he was crazy. But the son of a bitch pulled it off," Chang said with a slight laugh.

"You've known him since grad school?" Brandon said.

Chang nodded. "He and I go way back, yes. We're good friends, actually."

"What's he like?" Andy asked.

Chang paused, considering her words carefully. "He's brilliant…and very dedicated… A lot of people have their own opinions of him, so it's best to meet him in person to understand for yourself." She leaned back and glanced out the window behind her for a moment. "You're all very lucky," she began before turning back to them. "Not many people get to meet Billy in person these days, let alone work directly with him."

"Have you been to the reserve before?" Brandon asked.

Chang nodded. "Several times. It's absolutely breathtaking. You'll see soon enough."

As if on cue, the pilot turned around and shouted: "Final descent! ETA twenty minutes."

The executive glanced at her watch. "Excellent." She returned to her seat across from Jones, who was still gazing outside with the same blank stare.

Sydney turned back to her own window. The ground was starting to get closer.

The plane touched down atop a plateau about a hundred feet above the flat prairies. On each side of the tarmac was a gently sloping hill covered with trees. The landing itself was fairly rough; the entire aircraft shuddered violently and for a moment it seemed as if the very frame would buckle. Somehow, the pilot managed to come to a halt before the end of the short runway. Everyone looked frazzled as they unbuckled their seatbelts and stood up.

"I could've landed that better in my sleep," she heard Chang mutter.

"You're a pilot?" Sydney accidentally blurted out.

"Actually, yes. I mostly fly for recreation, but I did this route before a couple years ago." She glanced around the cabin. "Same plane."

The cabin door was located on the rear left side. The pilot moved past them to open it and folded out a short series of metal stairs. Once everyone had their backpacks, they climbed down and onto the tarmac. It was cooler than Sydney would have expected, a soft late afternoon breeze brushing the humidity away.

Three black men walked towards them. Two of them wore white polo shirts and shorts, but the other wore camo fatigues, Aviator sunglasses, and was extremely fit. He strode towards them with a sense of military formality.

"Ramsay," Chang said, walking towards him. "It's been a while."

He flashed a friendly smile but his sharp posture never faltered. With an unmistakably Kenyan accent, he said, "I hope you all had safe travels. These two" – he gestured to the men behind him – "will take care of your baggage and bring it to your rooms. I'd like to remind you that there is no cellular reception here, nor will you be having any contact with the outside world for the next two weeks. I also ask you to avoid taking pictures of our equipment or using your cameras in the laboratories. We conduct some very valuable research there and have many competitors. Now, if you'll follow me, Dr. Sans is waiting." He turned on his heel and started towards a break in the treeline.

They followed him and Sydney felt from the way he walked they should fall into a single file line. They reached the clearing's edge and she saw a paved trail leading down through the forest for a couple hundred feet or so. There appeared to be a building or structure beyond. A wooden sign to the right of the path read: "Welcome to Simba Kishindo Game Reserve."

"Lion's Roar," Andy muttered beside her, translating.

"Is that Swahili?" she asked. He nodded.

The buzzing of insects danced by their ears as they continued down through the forest. Finally, they came out into an open area with a manicured lawn and landscaping where a large safari lodge stood before them near the base of the hill. The wooden structure was two stories high with a roof made to look like straw, although there were several solar panels along it. Sydney could see a skylight over one area at the top. They approached the building and Ramsay led them straight towards a series of wide glass double-doors. Before he could open them, a man stepped out.

He looked a few years younger than forty-seven, which Sydney knew was his real age, with his golden blond hair slicked back. He was tall and fit, but not as muscular as Ramsay, and wore a hefty watch that she recognized as a Casio Pathfinder, popular amongst hunters and outdoorsmen. There was some kind of black sweatband around his right wrist. His eyes were a gleaming blue and he walked towards them with a wide smile – a genuine one, like the one she had seen in the photo of him with the lion.

He first went to Chang, who extended her hand until he gave her a full embrace. "It's been too long," he said with the hint of a British accent, patting her on the back. Then he turned to the interns. Sydney suddenly realized she was the closest to him and found his arm outstretched toward her.

"I'm Billy Sans. How do you do?"

TOUR

She shook his hand and noted the confidently firm grip. "I'm Sydney," she somehow managed to say without stuttering. Sans moved to shake Andy's next, then Brandon's and Courtney's.

Finally, he reached Jones, who appeared to regard him with suspicion. If he noticed this, Sans's didn't show it. "Richard, how are the kids?"

"Just fine, Billy," he said blankly. His eyes narrowed as Sans turned back to face the rest of them and clapped his hands together.

"I see you've already met my assistant Edward Ramsay, so let's start the tour." He turned and led them towards the open double doors. "Forgive me for being so excited, I rarely get visitors and there's so much to see."

They stepped inside and found themselves in a large

sitting room with wood-paneled walls and floor-to-ceiling bookcases. There was a painting of a Serengeti sunset mounted on an open space at the back wall. The chairs and sofas sported expensive-looking upholstery. There were two exits on the left and right from where they were standing, each appearing to lead down a different corridor.

"Here's the library," Sans said. "This is actually the rear of the house. The front entrance is this way." He led them through an open entryway on the left, then made a right turn and led them down a hallway.

They came out into a large foyer with a high ceiling. There was a grand staircase to their right leading up to the next floor; two large wooden doors stood before them. A large, diamond chandelier hung above the center of the room. Despite the furnishings and the clear inspiration from classic safari lodges, something about the design felt modern to Sydney. Everything was carefully arranged and there weren't too many ornate decorations, just the occasional painting of an animal on the walls and some framed photographs.

Looking closely at one next to her, she saw a young Sans, looking no older than seven, smiling while his parents crouched next to him on each side. They were out somewhere in the savanna and there was an old Land Rover behind them to the right. Below the picture but still framed behind the glass, "Christmas 1980" was written neatly with a sharpie. A few feet away, she saw another from when Sans was a teenager. He and his father, who had aged quite visibly, were standing over a dead lioness. This one was labeled "First Lion Kill – June 1989".

Sans had purposefully paused here to let everyone take it in. Then, he pointed to the staircase and continued: "That leads to the next level where all the bedrooms are as well as access to the balcony. Dinner will be served in here." He walked through an open space to the left.

They followed him into a dining room with large windows. The table was a thick rectangle of polished oak surrounded by ten chairs. There was a large mirror on the wall to the left. Out the windows, she could see an expansive patio and a large infinity pool with a great view stretching off into the distance.

"We'll get to that in a moment," Sans said, noticing most of their attentions had turned outside. He pointed to a door at the back of the room. "The kitchen is beyond there. Fatou, the chef, is excellent. He's currently preparing some wildebeest for tonight."

Sans moved back into the foyer and pointed down a hallway across from them. "That's the way to the garage and to the staff's living quarters. Now, if you'll follow me…" He started up the stairs. When they reached the landing, Sydney saw they were in a small open space with a set of wooden double doors directly ahead and two hallways branching off to each side. There were two tropical ferns potted and sitting on each side of the double doors.

"That's my office and bedroom," Sans said. He walked forward and spun around, his arms spread out in both directions of the corridors. "There are four guest rooms on each side of this floor, eight in total. Ellie, Richard, you'll get the east wing to yourselves." He pointed to his right. "And interns, you'll stock the west." He gestured in the other direction. "But we'll get to that later. This way."

They walked down the eastern hall past the four rooms, two on each side. At the end on the northern side was a glass door that led to a balcony. Sans held the door open for them as they stepped outside and took it all in. There was a straw-roof overhang providing shade for four lawn chairs. The balcony jutted out roughly fifteen feet and took up about one fourth of the width of the lodge. At the railing, Sydney looked down towards the patio and the water. There was a wooden path before the pool deck began that led from the front doors to each side of the building. There were two decently sized windmills located a hundred feet off each end of the lodge, and looking up towards the roof she saw it was lined with more solar panels.

"How long have you had this place?" Brandon asked.

"My parents bought it in 1972, about a year before I was born. This isn't the original lodge; I had it built about a decade ago. The old one was much smaller. And there was no pool." He glanced out at one of the wind turbines. "And it had a considerably larger carbon footprint."

"How large is the reserve?" Andy said.

"Nearly one hundred square miles," Sans replied. "We're in the southern portion here. The entire western edge borders Serengeti National Park, which you can reach going just over ten miles that way." He turned around and walked to the far end of the balcony. Ramsay hung back while the others went to the railing to get a better view of the north.

Sydney leaned out over the railing and gazed off at the plains, leveling her hand across her forehead to shield her eyes from the sunlight.

"I'm sure you're all ready to get out there, so why wait?" Sans said, glancing at his Pathfinder watch. "We've got about an hour until sunset." He turned around and looked at all of them with a wide smile. "Perfect time for a safari."

"Sir," Ramsay spoke up, a look of concern on his face. "I don't think we would be able to make it back before–"

Sans held up his hand and Ramsay went silent. "We'd better get going. Time is of the essence."

And he smiled.

SAFARI

The garage was a structure adjacent to the rest of the lodge. Bordering the building's east side, it housed five SUVs and swaths of field equipment on shelves along the back. The walls were a sparse white and the floor was smooth gray concrete, giving off a different aura than the resort-like quality of the areas they had seen earlier.

The vehicles were dark green Land Rover Discoveries, the sleeker variant from the 2017 model year onward, and had been retrofitted with forward-facing light rigs. The chassis of each SUV appeared to have a raised suspension and the wheels looked decisively more all-terrain than the standard model. Two at the far end appeared to have additional racks on the roofs and rear bumpers. Sydney also noticed they were all plugged in with their charging cords leading to several Tesla batteries on the eastern wall, another aftermarket feature.

Sans turned to an Afrikaner polo-shirted staff member and gestured to the two Rovers nearest to them. "We'll take these. Ramsay will drive one, you get the other." The staff member nodded and moved to the vehicle on the right while Sans climbed into the passenger seat of the one closest.

Ramsay opened the rear left door turned towards Sydney, motioning for her to get in. The interior had three rows of comfortable leather seats and industrial-grade floormats. She went in-between the second-row bucket seats and settled into a chair at the very back. There were two sunroofs, one over the driver and the front passenger, and a second over the rear two rows. Chang climbed into the row in front of her and Andy was about to follow, but seeing that Sans was in this car, Courtney abruptly brushed past him. Andy had no choice but to walk to the other vehicle and Sydney felt alone in the company of strangers.

Courtney shut the left rear door behind her as she sat down while Chang was already buckling herself in beside her. Sans waited until they were all secured, watching in the rear view mirror, before holding up a Motorola two-way radio and saying, "Okay Kobus, move out."

Two of the doors retracted open in front of the Rovers. The other SUV drove out first, then Ramsay pressed his foot on the accelerator and there was a soft electric whir as they rolled out of the building. There was a well-worn dirt path that led away from the garage and out into the savanna. Up in the sky, the sun gently drifted ever closer to the horizon and the heavens began their transition from late afternoon into dusk.

"We probably won't see many animals until we've crossed the river," Ramsay said over his shoulder.

Sydney peered between the rows of seats and saw a small forest of trees looming up ahead through the windshield. A few minutes later they had reached it and followed the other Land

Rover along another dirt trail. The tree cluster was bisected by a winding river, over which a wooden bridge had been constructed for vehicles to pass. Once across the water, they continued through the other half of the forest cluster before emerging back onto the prairies.

This area was much more expansive, in line with what Sydney had seen from the plane earlier. Looking up at the far reaches of the evening sky through the sunroof, the vastness of this place struck her full-force. Here she was in a vehicle dwarfed by an enormous ecosystem that was but a tiny fraction of the planet's surface. It was something to think about.

Suddenly, the vehicle came to a halt. Everyone was looking at something.

"There," Sans said, pointing.

Then she saw the animals.

Just about two hundred feet off to their left, a herd of elephants was bathing in a pond. The sunroofs retracted and the windows rolled down. "Binoculars are under the seats," Sans said.

Sydney retrieved a pair and then stood up through the sunroof. A cool evening breeze blew through her sandy blonde hair as she brought the binoculars up to her eyes. She watched as the animals sent water cascading down over their heads, then re-submerged their trunks for more. There seemed to be about twenty of them, relatively small for a herd. Sydney counted seven wading in the water while the rest either took mud baths on the shore or relaxed in the nearby grass.

They began to roll forward again and Sydney dropped back down into her seat. Chang was still looking at the elephants while Courtney tried to spot other animals out her window, scanning the landscape with her binoculars.

"Something's over there," she announced. Sydney leaned

over to get closer to the open window. Looking through her own set of field glasses, she saw a herd of wildebeest grazing off in the distance.

"Let's find something a little more exciting, shall we?" Sans said.

It was another five minutes before they spotted anything else. Chang pointed at something off to the left and Sydney climbed back up through the sunroof to spy a herd of Thomson's gazelle running through the fields. To her, there was something fascinating about the way the brown creatures undulated in and out of the tall grass, moving in unison like a school of fish.

By now, the sun was much lower in the sky. Sydney guessed they had no more than fifteen minutes left before it set.

Ramsay turned to Sans. "We'd better get back soon."

"It'll be fine."

"The dark–"

"I said it'll be *fine*," Sans hissed. It was the first time Sydney had noticed a change from his cheery mood, but he immediately regained it a second later as he looked back at the rest of them. "There's just something I'd still like us to see…"

Ten minutes later, beneath the last vestiges of the twilight, Sydney climbed up to the sunroof with the others and brought the binoculars to her eyes once more.

"Can you see them?" Sans was asking.

"I think…there, yes I see them!" Courtney said. "My god, they're beautiful."

Chang was silent but smiling as she gazed on with her own lenses. She clearly saw them too. Sydney didn't, and as she frantically swept the landscape, her shoulders tensed up. If she wasn't careful, she would miss–

There.

Just over five hundred feet away, a lioness raised her head. For a moment, she gave Sydney a great view of her majestic profile, then the animal looked towards the Land Rover and the sunset briefly glinted off one of her golden eyes. She wasn't alone either. Sydney saw several others in the grass nearby, including a male with its magnificent mane.

"How'd you know we'd find them?" Chang asked.

Beside her, Sans pointed down to the GPS on the console screen as he leaned against the frame of the vehicle. "All the animals here are embedded with microchips. None of our views this evening were by chance."

Far away, the orange sun slipped beneath the plains.

Ramsay climbed up from his seat and turned to Sans. "Sir, we need to leave *now*."

Sans looked back in the direction of the lions without answering. Then after a moment, he silently nodded, his expression completely calm. Ramsay got back into the driver's seat and the Land Rover turned around, heading south. The second car, twenty feet away, followed suit. Sydney watched the pride through her binoculars for as long as she could, then she dropped back into her seat and relaxed the rest of the way back, taking in the cool evening breeze as it flowed in through the sunroofs and the windows.

The vehicles pulled into the garage just as the remaining faint glimpses of light faded from the sky.

FEAST

The dining room had already been prepared when they arrived. The table was set with silverware and wine glasses; two unopened bottles of champagne sat in ice buckets beside a few baskets of bread. Outside the windows, the night was too dark to see anything. Sans took a seat at the head of the table with Chang and Ramsay joining him on either side. Sydney sat between Chang and Andy and across from Courtney while Brandon sat across from Andy. Jones found himself alone beside Brandon.

A servant emerged from the kitchen, dressed in a white uniform, and filled their glasses with water from a steel pitcher.

Sans folded his hands on the table and said, "Thank you all for coming. I occasionally get zoologists that come in and stay for a few days or a few of my old hunting friends, but for the most part it gets quite lonely here." He smiled, almost as if were a joke.

"Then how come you never leave?" came a voice from the other end of the table. Sydney turned to see Jones staring at him with a steely gaze.

Sans seemed caught off guard by the remark. His eyes narrowed and his head tilted quizzically for a brief moment, then he laughed it off. "You've all seen the natural wonders I have at my fingertips every day. If you had access to that, would you ever leave?"

Sydney realized she probably wouldn't.

"Lacking a good reason, of course," Sans added.

"I can think of several," Jones said, forcing a smile.

Sans's brow furrowed. "Then perhaps later you can enlighten me." He turned his attention to the interns. "Everything we do here is one hundred percent powered by renewable energy. You've seen the wind turbines, perhaps a few of you even glimpsed the solar panels mounted on the roof. Contrary to popular belief, I'm very committed to sustainability and the environment. Last year, the Sans Conservation Fund donated a million dollars to Serengeti National Park."

Another server came out and opened one of the champagne bottles. He started around the table, pouring the women's glasses first, then the men's ending with Sans as they continued talking.

"How does that conflict with hunting?" Jones asked. "I mean, isn't that the very thing all the eco-warriors want to stop?"

Now he appeared to be getting on Sans's nerves. "That's a common mistake, actually. I'm almost disappointed that someone of your intellect would fall for such a rampant misconception, Richard. Hunting isn't damaging to the ecosystem. *Poaching* is the illegal killing of protected animals and it is very much a problem that we environmentalists are trying to stop, yes. *Hunting* is a sport. It requires permits, licenses. It is measured. And in many cases, it assists population control during a natural predator-prey imbalance. Besides, what I hunt here has no bearing beyond this reserve." He smiled. "All my animals are cloned."

"All of them?" Courtney asked, stunned.

Sans nodded. "We started growing them here in artificial wombs about five years ago as a proof of concept for investors. All the DNA was taken from species in captivity. Now those same technologies are being put towards everything from new limbs for amputees to optimized dog breeding."

"You said you grew them here?" Andy asked.

"At the veterinary lab building. It's a few hundred feet that way." He gestured behind him. "You probably couldn't see it from the patio earlier because it's obscured by trees. But that's where all the scientific research around here gets done. The facilities are state-of-the-art. You'll see soon enough; each of you will be doing some work there over the next two weeks."

"Forgive me," Jones said. "But even if they're clones, I don't see how that justifies killing them for fun. They're still living things, after all."

Sans sipped his champagne. "Hunting is not about slaughtering animals or satisfying a bloodlust, it's about the challenge. I apologize for the cliché, but it's the *thrill*, the *excitement* that makes it unique. Your life is on the line and suddenly everything you've been raised with – academics, social skills, you name it – aren't going to help you. It taps into a different part of the brain, the primal survival instincts we've buried deep in our subconscious. Every day, we deny they're there. Hunting, big-game hunting, is one of the few activities on Earth that still has the power to remind us what we really are."

"And what's that?" Chang asked, holding her glass.

"Predators." He glanced around the table. "I can see there's some uneasiness here. Let me clarify: *Homo sapiens* is a predatory species. Look no further than these." He pointed towards his eyes with two fingers. "Notice how they are forward-facing. Just like a lion's, just like a wolf's, or a bear's, or an eagle's. Have you ever wondered why herbivorous animals such as deer and gazelle have their eyes towards the side of their heads? It's so they can more easily spot an attack coming. Predators have their vision facing forward to track their prey. We are built for the offensive."

Several servants came out of the kitchen carrying plates while a black man wearing a chef's hat, who Sydney guessed must be Fatou, oversaw their actions. As one was put down in front of her, she saw it was cooked wildebeest with sides of rice and green beans neatly arranged on the bone china's surface.

Sans continued talking as they returned to the kitchen to retrieve more plates. "Despite our species hunting for food for ninety-nine percent of our existence, you've no doubt heard some stuck-up asshole tell you we are now more *evolved* than that. Take a quick look at the latest trends and you'll clearly see we're not."

He didn't even bother looking at his plate when it was placed before him. "What really irks me is that people constantly rail against hunting, yet give eco-tourism a pass. I suppose it makes sense; hunting is an easy target and people just want to feel good about themselves regardless of them actually making a difference or not. And yet all over the world, people travel to places of natural beauty from Africa to Costa Rica to the Great Barrier Reef and wind up damaging and disrupting the ecosystem just to catch a glimpse of some rare animals. This creates entire industries of people developing land in these areas and driving boats out to reefs, which all wind up destroying habitats, polluting them, or otherwise impacting the migration patterns of thousands of species – but one fucking dentist shoots a lion and the entire goddamn Internet gets set ablaze!"

The *z* at the end came out with a lisp. Sans suddenly clenched up, squeezing his eyes tightly. He muttered something under his breath but all Sydney could make out was "...*stupid, fucking...*" before he snapped out of it and returned to a more amicable demeanor. "Clearly I haven't had enough wine yet."

Everyone began eating their food and small talk broke out in groups. The rest of the meal passed uneventfully, but Sydney saw Jones silently glancing at Sans from time to time with an uneasy look.

After dinner, Ramsay took the interns upstairs to show them to their rooms; Sans, Chang, and Jones needed to discuss "business". Sydney's was located at the northwestern corner and had a queen-sized bed, a mahogany desk, and a bathroom. There were also two windows, one facing north and the other west. Her suitcase had been brought in by the staff earlier and now sat on the bed.

The first thing she did was move it to the desk and lie down atop the sheets, all the jet lag from earlier swiftly returning. It had vaporized during her initial excitement of arriving at the lodge and the subsequent safari, but now all she could think of was sleep.

She figured she should at least brush her teeth and found the willpower to get up and shuffle over to the desk. After finding her toothbrush in her toiletry kit, she turned to walk to the bathroom when something caught her eye out of the western window.

Curious, Sydney went over and pressed her face against the glass pane, trying to make out anything in the black night. Off through some nearby trees, she could discern the lights of a building. After a moment, she realized it must be the veterinary lab that Sans was talking about earlier. Still, something seemed odd about it, like a series of disembodied illuminations in the forest. Were people working there at this hour?

She needed some sleep. Turning away from the window,

she headed to the bathroom to get ready for bed. A few minutes later she turned off the lights and tucked herself under the sheets. She was dozing off when a strange noise reached her ears and her eyes flashed open.

It had come from the north. She couldn't be certain, but it had sounded like the roar of a lion – but not like any kind of lion she'd ever heard. The pitch seemed off and it sounded unnerving, chilling her to the bone. Even stranger, it sounded fairly close by.

FIELD WORK

"Today, the real fun begins," Sans said, walking into the dining room just as Sydney took another sip of orange juice. "I hope nobody's too jet lagged."

She had slept like a rock and had woken up at 8:30. Realizing she had slept for nearly eleven hours, she had quickly gotten dressed and ran downstairs to see that breakfast was already being served: scrambled eggs and toast. Andy, Courtney, and Brandon were already there.

"Only a little," Courtney joked.

"We have plenty of coffee if anyone needs it. After you've eaten, you'll be split into two pairs. One will head out into the field every day to insert the latest microchip iteration into the animals, the other will work in the lab to analyze the field data as it comes in. Then next week, you'll switch positions." Sans glanced at his watch. "I've got a call in five minutes. I'll catch you around later."

He turned and left the room as Ramsay walked in, stopping at the end of the table with his trademark military posture. "Sydney, Brandon, you'll be on the tagging operation with me this week. Dress for the outdoors and come to the garage; it's over eighty degrees outside. Andy, Courtney, you'll meet Dr. Makimba in the foyer and she'll take you to the laboratory building. Get where you're supposed to be in ten minutes." He walked off.

As she finished her breakfast, Sydney felt nervous. She had hoped she'd be put with Andy in the event of a pairing; she barely knew Brandon at all. She drained the last of her orange juice and returned upstairs to her room.

Now dressed in boots, khaki shorts, and a safari jacket over a white tank top, Sydney entered the garage to see Ramsay and Brandon next to the nearest Land Rover, talking to a stern-looking red-haired woman wearing dark blue scrubs.

Brandon saw her and held up a small pill bottle as she walked over. "Guess what Sydney? We get more meds!" There was a heavy dose of sarcasm in his voice.

In a similar tone, she said, "Oh joy," as a smile came to her face. *Maybe this won't be so bad after all.*

Ramsay gestured to the woman beside him. "This is Nurse Graves. She's here to give both of you your new antimalarial medication."

"But I'm already on doxycycline," she said, looking between them. "I started taking it two days before we left the States."

"Yes, but doxycycline makes you highly susceptible to sun exposure, which wouldn't be suitable for your field work this week, now would it?" Graves said. Something about the way she talked reminded Sydney of a patronizing teacher she'd had in the sixth grade.

"I guess not," she said as the nurse handed her the container. She glanced it over in her hands. The label read:

PRIMAQUINE PHOSPHATE
TABLETS, USP
23.6 mg (=15 mg base)
Rx ONLY
15 tablets

She'd heard of primaquine before. It was one of the most common drugs used for malaria prevention. Ramsay held out a steel-gray water bottle with the SansCorp logo emblazoned on the side. "Take it with this," he said. She took out one of the round tablets and popped it into her mouth, swallowing it with a swig from the bottle.

"Excellent," Graves said, grabbing the pills out of her hand. She made her way over to Brandon to collect his. "I'll leave these in your rooms. Make sure to take one every morning after breakfast. You might get an upset stomach if you take it without food."

As the nurse headed for the door back to the rest of the lodge, Ramsay turned his attention to a silver case sitting on the hood of the Land Rover. He opened it up to reveal some kind of sleek medical injector gun sitting atop padded white foam. "This is the transmission mechanism for the new Mark VII chips, which are here." He pointed to ten slots in the foam with cylindrical metal devices each no bigger than a grain of rice. "They are to be placed at the back of the neck along the spinal cord, and are much better at monitoring impulses along the central nervous system than the Mark VIs. All the information gets directly transmitted to our computers in the vet labs, where your friends will be monitoring it all week. First, the animal has to be tranquilized. That will be my job. Then I will show you how to perform the procedure."

He closed up the case. "There's sunblock in the car. You're going to need it."

Sydney stared out the window at the passing plains as she slathered Neutrogena SPF 70 onto the back of her neck. She was excited to be getting back out into the savanna. The wonders of last evening's safari were still fresh on her mind.

"After all those shots we got before the trip, here I was thinking we were done," Brandon joked.

"I guess it's better to be safe than sorry."

"True. I'm just worried about the side effects. With all these vaccines and medications over a short time, the likelihood that they'll interact is quite high."

"What kind of side effects?" she asked.

"Just about everything from mild nausea to death." He smiled.

"Hopefully not," she laughed. "I'd like to keep enjoying this place."

He looked out his window. "It really is quite something…"

Ramsay pointed to the touch-panel on the center console. "Those red dots are gazelle. Those are what we're going after first."

A few minutes later, he parked the car under the shade of an acacia tree and retracted the sunroofs. In the passenger seat was a long-range tranquilizer rifle. Ramsay stood up through the opening and rested the gun on the roof's lighting rig. Sydney and Brandon climbed up to the rear sunroof to get a better look.

"Do you see them?" Ramsay asked, looking through the scope.

Even without her binoculars, Sydney could. They were

about three hundred feet up ahead, a herd of gazelle grazing amongst the grass.

"They haven't noticed us?" she asked.

"Electric vehicles don't make much noise and we're downwind. Besides, they don't usually care. Until this happens." There was a *pfft* and the gun buckled. Off in the field, she saw one of the gazelle abruptly stop grazing and run around before collapsing. The rest scattered, fleeing farther out into the prairie as Ramsay rapidly loaded another dart into the chamber.

Brandon ducked down and came back up with a pair of binoculars to watch them run while Ramsay lined up another shot.

"Do you need to be closer to–?" she began.

The gun jolted again. Brandon peered closer into the lenses for a moment, then said, "It's down."

Ramsey brought the weapon down and turned to them, a smile on his face. "It's more fun out of the car. And with real bullets."

He lowered himself back into the driver's seat and moments later the Land Rover was cruising towards the first of the two sedated animals, each marked by unmoving red dots on the screen while the rest had fled out of the viewing area.

About ten feet away from the first gazelle, Ramsay stopped the vehicle, grabbed the case from the floor beside him, and got out of the car. Sydney and Brandon followed suit. She could see the rising and falling of the creature's chest as it lay on its side. It was barely over three feet long, had two horns on its head relatively close together, and most of its body was covered by brown fur; however, there was a horizontal black streak around the middle of each side that gave way to a white underbelly. A tranquilizer dart was embedded in its neck.

"Good shot," Brandon noted.

"Thank you." Ramsay crouched beside the animal and opened the case on the ground, then held up the injector. "Who wants to go?"

Brandon stepped aside and gestured for Sydney to come forward. "Ladies first," he said, spoken like a true Southern gentleman.

She crouched down beside Ramsay as he held up one of the chips for her to see. It appeared to be a smaller, more advanced version of the Radio Frequency Identification (RFID) tags they placed in household pets, although those were inserted with special syringes. Most field researchers used collars or directly-attached transmitters for wildlife tracking due to concerns that the signal strength of implanted GPS chips were affected by the animal's body mass, but Sydney knew that SansCorp had spent the last several years marketing advanced RFID tech with bolstered signals. She also knew Simba Kishindo was used as a private testing ground for the company's new zoology tech and guessed the Mark VII devices were still prototypes.

"You insert it into the injector like this," Ramsay was saying, feeding the chip into an opening slot at the top of the gun. There was only room for one chip at a time and he slid a flap over the chamber after the tiny cylinder clicked in. "Then you find the base of the neck."

With his left hand, he felt around the top of the animal's shoulders. Then his hand froze in position and brought the gun around, as if prepared to inject the syringe of the device through a patch of skin between his thumb and his index finger. However, he stopped short of doing so and handed it to Sydney.

"Now you do it," he said.

She took the injector into her hand. It was no bigger than the size of an average pistol and weighed only a few pounds. Ramsay moved back a few feet but still leaned in to supervise. Brandon came around to the other side as her left hand stroked the back of the gazelle's neck, drifting gently down towards to shoulder blades as she felt along the vertebrae. Then, picking a spot, she placed her thumb and index finger about an inch apart to spread the fur and readied the injector.

"One last thing," Ramsay said, raising a finger. "Make sure the chip doesn't directly go into the spinal column."

"That would probably be bad," Brandon joked.

Sydney carefully moved the injector into position against the animal's skin and pulled the trigger. There was the sound of pressurized air being released and she briefly saw something silver fly down the clear syringe tube and burrow itself into the flesh. When she moved the device away, she saw a tiny wound no more than a quarter of an inch wide.

"Excellent," Ramsay said.

"How long before the tranquilizer wears off?" she asked.

"About half an hour." Ramsay looked off in the direction of the other gazelle, about a hundred feet away. "Brandon, you'll do the next one."

As the hot sun beat down from above, they walked over through the tall grass and repeated the procedure on the second animal without any complications.

"There," Brandon said, standing up. "All in a day's work."

Ramsay laughed. "See those?" He pointed to the remaining eight RFID chips in the case. "Those are all just for today."

He told them that they would go after some wildebeest next. He explained that Sans wanted to roll the Mark VIIs out slowly in a just few members of each species, making sure everything was working before completing an entire sweep of the reserve. After that, they would break for lunch with some sandwiches that were packed in a cooler in the trunk. They started driving towards the northeast and soon arrived in an area where a cluster of unmoving GPS signals sat on the display.

And that was when Sydney spotted the carcasses.

REMAINS

"What the hell?" Brandon said as Ramsay brought the Land Rover to a halt.

Through the windshield, the remains of seven horribly mutilated wildebeest were strewn around a fifty-foot wide area. Several hyenas were currently feasting on the leftovers, but some of them turned their heads toward the vehicle to look at the new arrival, blood dripping from their jowls.

Ramsay reached for the glove compartment and pulled out a revolver. He held it up through the sunroof and loosed off two shots into the air. Frightened, the hyenas scattered. Keeping the gun by his side, Ramsay opened the door.

"This is the side of nature zoos don't show you," he said, climbing out of the car.

An unsettling feeling gripped Sydney as she exited the

SUV and closed the door behind her. All was quiet save for the wind as she proceeded towards the gruesome slaughter. She stopped next to where Ramsay was crouching to examine the ground. Brandon came up behind them.

She looked around. The animals were torn open and missing varying amounts of flesh, shredded innards distributed along the ground. Clouds of flies danced around the carcasses and a rotting odor wafted into Sydney's nose, making her stomach feel queasy. She was glad she hadn't eaten lunch yet.

"What did this?" Brandon asked. "A lion?"

Ramsay was still scanning the ground for tracks. "No."

Sydney racked her brain for knowledge of anything like this. It didn't remind her of any predator behavior she'd ever studied before. Hyenas were known to occasionally hunt in packs, but they weren't capable of something like this, so those ones had certainly been scavengers. Cheetahs didn't seem likely either. The wounds had clearly been inflicted by a big animal – several, more likely. The only thing she could think of was lions. But with prey as large as a wildebeest, lions would usually single out a weak member of a herd and work together to bring it down. It was just like that display of the two lionesses attacking the buffalo in the museum. That didn't fit this M.O. either.

The others had walked out into the midst of the carnage while Sydney pondered the scene. Brandon beckoned her closer. "Take a look at this," he said.

She came over and bent down to see a series of imprints on the ground. The creature that made them had four toes and paws almost half a foot across. Glancing around, she saw several different bloodstained trails moving around the bodies.

"Well, we're not going to be tagging these," Ramsay said, starting to walk back to the car.

"We can't just leave yet," Brandon said. "We don't know what did this."

"It was most likely lions," Ramsay called back over his shoulder.

"But you were sure it wasn't," Sydney said. Ramsay didn't hear her. She turned to Brandon, who was still looking around. "You heard him say that earlier, right? I mean, these couldn't have been lions. The behavior's all wrong. Could they have been crazy or infected with some kind of rabies?"

"Or on hard drugs," Brandon said, scratching the back of his head. "Honestly, I don't know what to make of this."

"Are you two coming?" Ramsay's voice shouted. The driver's side door was open and he already had one foot in the car.

She heard buzzing and slapped her neck, her hand coming away with the broken body of a large fly. There was blood on her palm and she grimaced.

Brandon took one final glance around, then started back for the Land Rover. Wiping her hand on her shorts, Sydney joined him. Once they were seated in the second row again, Ramsay turned the wheel and the vehicle set off in a different direction. Sydney looked out the back window for a while, staring at the crimson-stained grass and the motionless figures until they dwindled from sight.

LIBRARY

Late in the afternoon, Sydney walked into the lodge's library ready to curl up on one of the leather sofas with the Michael Crichton novel currently tucked under her arm. It had been a tiring day, but nothing else unusual had happened after the discovery of the carcasses. In total, she and Brandon had implanted chips in six more animals from giraffes to an elephant.

Ramsay had decided it was enough for the first day even though there were two left in the case. Besides, it had been getting hotter to the point where just standing outside the car had made everyone break into a sweat. It was supposed to be a similar temperature tomorrow, which she wasn't exactly thrilled about.

She was about to open to the last page she'd read as she moved towards the sofa, when she spotted the titles on the nearest bookshelf and, feeling curious, decided to take a closer look. At first, she saw some classics of science fiction from Jules Verne's *20,000 Leagues Under the Sea* to H.G. Wells's *The Island of Dr. Moreau.* The titles got more modern as she looked down the shelves from Ray Bradbury to William Gibson.

But the next bookcase over was dedicated entirely to works on Africa and hunting. Names of adventurers like Selous, Roosevelt, and Stanley were written on the sides of volumes worn with time and use. She even recognized John Henry Patterson's *The Man-Eaters of Tsavo*, about two killer lions whose bodies were now preserved at the Chicago Field Museum. There had been a Val Kilmer movie based on it called *The Ghost and the Darkness*, which she'd watched several times as a kid.

Sydney also noticed numerous works by a Peter Hathaway Capstick. She pulled one off the shelf titled *Death in the Long Grass* and looked it over, slipping her Crichton book back under her arm. It was hardcover and a male lion partially obscured by tall grass stared at her from the front flap. The back displayed the black and white photo of a man in safari attire seated next to jungle foliage. A hunting rifle rested in his lap and a fedora dangled from his hands.

"That's my favorite by him." Startled, she abruptly spun around to see Sans standing on the other side of the room.

"Oh, I'm sorry if I'm not allowed to—"

Sans put up his hand and walked over, eyeing the book as he went. "No problem at all. This place isn't off limits." He tapped the photo of the man on the rear flap. "Interesting character. Capstick started out as a stock broker, of all things. Pretty successful at it too. Then one day he decided enough was enough and dedicated his life to his passion. He went everywhere from the African savanna to South American rainforests, serving as a guide and a big-game hunter. Then he retired to Florida and continued to write about it. May I?"

"Sure," she said, realizing how soft her voice sounded as

she handed him the book. Other than a few tears on the jacket, it was in good shape.

"This was my father's copy," he said, turning it over. He opened the front cover and pointed to a name written in neat black pen: Gerard Sans. "If you think I'm into hunting, you should've seen him. Old bastard must've thought he was the next Frederick Selous. In his last days, I think he'd even had fantasies of dying during some epic Serengeti escapade."

"What happened to him?"

"Lung cancer," Sans said. He didn't look up but there was a more measured tone in his voice. "Got him fairly early at age sixty, but he puffed a pack a day no matter what continent he was standing on. It's why I don't smoke. Never have, never will. Then my mother died a few years later of liver failure. She'd always been a heavy drinker. Evidently, vices aren't my family's strong suit." He managed a smile.

Sydney felt glum. "I'm sorry…"

"Thank you, but they died in the 90s, nearly thirty years ago." He opened the book and flipped through a few pages. "Ah yes, the beginning passage here is my favorite. It's a true story about this big-game hunter on his final expedition. He's in Zambia, the Eastern Province, and his tent is far away from everybody else's. It's three AM, and while he's sleeping, this starving lioness creeps up through the darkness, sensing him in his slumber. And when she finally gets him, we reach the best line: 'For Peter Hankin, one of central Africa's most experienced professional white hunters, the last safari is over'."

Sans savored the words for a moment. "I still remember that sentence from when my dad read it to me for the first time. I was seven. He taught me everything I know about this sport. That line, he said, is what he lived for. The idea that hunting returned us to the natural world, a place where death could come at a moment's notice – and that's just the way it was. It was the feeling that your number could be up at any given second that made you feel the most alive." He paused, clearly thinking about something.

Then he handed the book back to her and she noticed he was wearing an orange sweatband around his right wrist today, as opposed to black the day before. "Feel free to read anything in here that you like."

And he walked back out the way he came.

After dinner, Sydney fetched the novel from her room and headed back down stairs. She'd spent the time after Sans left reading through some of the hunting books and before she'd known it, Ramsay had come in and asked her to come to the dining room. Now though, she wanted to do what she'd originally gone to the library for; she'd stopped reading at an interesting part.

But as she approached the corner that led into the library, she heard something and stopped in her tracks.

"…little project of his is blowing through funds faster than we can afford," Jones was saying. "And where are the results?"

Now Chang's voice: "Billy knows what he's doing. He's gotten the company out of tight spots before."

"But Ellie, we don't have time. The board's patience for him is wearing thinner by the day. In their mind, all he ever does now is fuck around out here."

"They can't touch him. He's the CEO, Chairman, and the largest single shareholder."

"Yes, they can," Jones said. "They can force a board vote. SansCorp's future is at stake, here."

"The company has its fingers in many pies. Revenue has been stable. And soon enough this venture will pay off, too. You don't know Billy like I do. He has…unique methods, but he always pulls through."

There was silence for a moment. Sydney pressed her body tightly to the corner and leaned towards the open frame of the entrance as much as she could without letting her head be visible to them inside.

"I don't know…," Jones finally said. "It just feels like he's not telling us everything. I'd like to see what goes on at that laboratory building, the stuff he doesn't let visitors see. I looked at the blueprints back in D.C., there's some kind of entrance to it from a cave about half a mile into the reserve."

Suddenly, the book slipped from Sydney's fingers and landed on the wooden floor with a *thunk*.

"What was that?" she heard Chang say.

Sydney quickly scooped the novel off the floor and slipped back towards the foyer as fast as she could.

HEAT

It must have been nearly ninety degrees as Sydney stepped out of the Land Rover the next day, but she'd been burning up long before she set foot outside. Her forehead had been hot to the touch from the moment she'd woken up, her body feeling tired and sore. Not wanting the anyone to think little of her, she took a refreshingly cold shower and drank several cups of coffee at breakfast.

That made her feel better for a short while, but the fever returned full force as she rode out to the plains with Ramsay and Brandon for another day of tagging. And the damned heat certainly wasn't helping.

Walking around to the back of the vehicle, she opened the trunk. Ramsay had placed the injector case in here today, next to several first aid kits in the event of an emergency. Sydney briefly thought about opening one up to see if it had aspirin or Tylenol or just about anything that would make the fever go away.

She pulled the silver case out, accidentally knocking over one of the kits in the process. It tumbled to the ground.

"Watch what you're doing," Brandon said, coming around the other side. "This shit's expensive."

"Sorry," she said, picking it up and putting a hand to her forehead. "I'm not feeling well."

"Are you sick?"

"I think so."

"Christ, then don't touch the case." He grabbed it out of her hand. "You're gonna infect all of us," he muttered, storming off.

What the hell is his problem? Sydney thought. *Someone woke up on the wrong side of the bed today...*

At that moment, she was more concerned with whatever she was coming down with. It was strange. She was unmistakably sick but had no cough, sore throat, or runny nose. There was just a painful ache creeping through her body that she couldn't quite put her finger on. And a splitting migraine. Could it have been a side effect of the vaccines, or the medicine perhaps? Something else?

She opened the first aid kit quickly and frantically searched around for painkillers.

"Sydney, are you coming?" she heard Brandon call off in the distance.

"Just a minute, asshole," she muttered. There were gauze bandages, alcoholic wipes, even nickel-plated scissors but no aspirin.

"Fuck." Now her head was really killing her, but she knew she had to get out there. *Not like my future depends on this or anything*, she thought.

She pressed the button inside the trunk for the door to

automatically close and began making her way to where Ramsay stood scanning the surroundings, the revolver held closely at his side. Brandon was already there, loading a chip into the injector.

"Do you see any others?" she asked as she got closer.

"No," Ramsay said, doing a final sweep. "She must've been hunting alone. They do that from time to time."

On the ground before her lay a tranquilized lioness. Ramsay had spotted her when they were tracking a zeal of zebras. He'd immediately grabbed the rifle and climbed through the sunroof, a rare look of genuine excitement on his face. Sydney and Brandon had initially been confused, then they'd managed to spot the predator as she slinked towards the herbivores about fifty feet away from a stray zebra. Through her binoculars, Sydney had watched as the huntress wheeled around when the dart hit her, looking everywhere to spot the attacker. She'd then turned her head towards the Land Rover and stared at them before finally lying down, her initial commotion having scared off the zebras.

"Damn, it's hot out here," she murmured, massaging her temples.

"Same as yesterday, really," Ramsay said, adjusting his aviators.

That was strange. She was sure it was warmer. It had to be. She felt buffeted on all sides by sweltering heat, feeling it seep through her pores at the same time as a second fire threatened to explode inside her head.

Brandon crouched beside the lioness and felt around the base of the neck, moving the injector in with his other hand. Her mind in a daze, the only thing Sydney could concentrate on was the creature itself. The entire rest of the world seemed to fall away save for the animal. As she stared at the five-and-a-half-foot long predator, all she could think of were the eviscerated wildebeest from the day before and the imprints on the ground. She glanced at one of the lioness's front paws; it looked similar enough, she guessed.

Sydney watched Brandon finish up with the implant and realized Ramsay was looking at her. "Are you alright?" he asked.

"Just a little under the weather. I'll be fine."

"Hold on," he said, coming closer. He put the base of his wrist to her forehead. "You need to see a nurse. We're going back."

"Going back?" Brandon said, looking almost angry. "We can't go back just because of her!"

"I'll drop her off with the nurse, then we can come back out later," Ramsay explained calmly.

"Good," Brandon grunted. "I don't want her to hold us back."

Had she been feeling even slightly better, she probably would have asked what the fuck was wrong with him today but she could barely concentrate with the searing heat inside her skull.

Ramsay led them back to the vehicle. *Why the hell is it so hot out here?* she thought. Ninety had to be an underestimate; there was no way it wasn't at least a hundred degrees today. The sun shot beams of heat directly down onto her and the air felt thick with humidity.

Somehow she managed to climb back into her seat and do up the seatbelt. The windows were rolled down and cool wind blew across her face. It made her feel better, but only for a moment until she realized something.

Most of the heat was coming from within her.

It seemed to take forever to get back. After they'd parked in front of the garage, Ramsay walked her across the front patio by the pool and through the forest towards the veterinary building. Even in her fevered state, she realized this was the first time she was seeing it properly. It was a new-looking postmodern structure, rectangularly shaped with large glass pane windows. It seemed to be roughly half the size of the lodge.

Ramsay led her along a paved trail towards two steel doors beneath a sign with dark lettering that read: SANSCORP LABORATORIES – SIMBA KISHINDO.

"This is very official-looking," she muttered in a daze.

"Some very expensive research goes on here," Ramsay explained. The doors retracted as they approached.

Inside, the colors of the walls were white and blue and everything had a sanitized, clean atmosphere. There were two hallways and Ramsay took her down the one to the left towards a door marked RITA GRAVES.

He opened it without knocking. The nurse was sitting behind a small desk, looking something over on an iPad. She looked up as they walked in and flashed an insincere smile.

"What's the problem?"

"I don't feel well," Sydney mumbled, putting a hand to her head.

"She's got a fever," Ramsay elaborated. "A bad one."

"Let's see how bad it is," Graves said, retrieving a thermometer from her desk and standing up. She placed it in Sydney's ear, waited for the beep, then glanced at the display. Her expression turned sour. "Thirty-nine point six. Not good."

Sydney feebly tugged at Ramsay's arm. "What's that in Fahrenheit?"

"Over a hundred and three," Graves said, putting on latex gloves and pulling a sheet of paper across an exam table at the back of the room. "I've seen worse, but we better check her out just in case." She turned around and patted the paper. "Sit here."

Sydney ambled over and managed to pull herself up, realizing that her muscles felt sorer than earlier. The nurse grabbed an otoscope from its charging station on her desk and turned back to her. "Open wide," she said.

Sydney opened her mouth as Graves shone the light around the back of her throat. "I don't see any inflammation." She checked Sydney's ears next. "Seems normal."

She turned back to the desk to return the otoscope. Ramsay was leaning against the wall, his arms folded. "Where do you feel it?" Graves asked.

"My head hurts," she said, massaging her temples.

"How so?"

"Like it's burning… Sorry, I don't know how to describe it exactly."

"Anything else?" Graves asked.

"My muscles are aching all over."

"As in arms, legs, abdomen…"

She nodded.

"And when did you first start having these symptoms?"

"This morning, when I woke up."

The nurse bit her lip, thinking. "You took your medication today?"

"Yes."

"Good." She eyed Sydney quizzically. "But this isn't malaria. The only thing I can think of with the muscle pain and fever would be Dengue."

"But I had a shot for that," she said feebly, rubbing her eye with the back of her wrist.

"Exactly. So, here's what we're going to do. I'm going to give you a fever reducer and you're going to take the rest of the afternoon off."

Sydney had no objections to that.

Graves gave her two aspirin and Ramsay brought in a paper cup of water for her to take them with. As he escorted her back to the building's entrance, a thought flashed through her mind amidst the pain of her fever. It was something she'd overheard Jones say the night before about this place. Something about there being things here that she wasn't allowed to see.

RECOVERY

Sydney reclined on a lawn chair in a shady area of the patio beneath the balcony. Her eyes registered words on the pages of the novel in her lap, but her brain was still too frazzled to piece together the meanings of each paragraph. Sighing, she put the book down yet again and looked out at the pool.

The painkillers had worked, but she still felt sore and unimaginably tired. The first thing she'd done when she got back to her room was to take a cold shower and nap for several hours. She'd missed lunch during that time but had no appetite anyway, so she didn't mind.

Knowing that if she slept more she'd never get to sleep tonight, Sydney decided to take up reading by the pool for some fresh air. She was now wearing shorts and a t-shirt; her flip flops sat on the patio beside her.

"Not feeling well, are we?" Andy's voice said behind her.

"Never better," she said, forcing a smile. "What day is it?"

"July fifteenth."

"I meant the day of the week."

"Wednesday. We got here Monday afternoon, remember?"

"Right," she said, rubbing her eyes.

"Seriously though, are you alright?"

"I think I just need to stay lying down for a bit."

"Mind if I pull up a chair?"

"Go for it."

Andy brought a nearby lawn chair closer, then sat down and folded his hands in his lap. "Sorry if I haven't been talking to you as much lately. I was hoping you'd make some new friends." He grinned. "Foolish, I know. How's Brandon?"

"He seemed pretty nice yesterday and I don't know what happened, but today he was a total douchebag."

Andy stared out at the pool. "You've always had a great effect on people."

"If my brain didn't feel like it was going to melt, I'd punch you on the arm."

"I'll consider myself punched." He grinned again and she rolled her eyes. "Hey, maybe he's just not feeling well either."

"I think it was more than just that. I mean, it came out of nowhere. It was a complete personality whiplash."

"Maybe he'll be better tomorrow."

"I hope," she said.

"Any idea what you've come down with?"

"Not a clue. I had every vaccination under the sun. The nurse said she didn't know what to make of it."

"What are your symptoms?"

"It's weird," Sydney said. "I've got no sore throat, no cough or anything like that, but I had a one hundred and three-degree fever and there's this dull pain throughout my entire body."

Andy scratched his chin. "Sounds like a party. And you just started feeling like this today?"

"This morning, yeah."

"Did you come into contact with anything contaminated recently? Maybe you ate something?"

"No and my stomach feels fine. Maybe it's just a side effect of the vaccines." She rubbed her forehead. "Anyway, enough of that. How's the analytic stuff going? Is Courtney tolerable?"

"You know, she's really not that bad. She just comes off as a bit bossy sometimes." He thought for a moment. "Do you mind if I say something?"

She shrugged. "I'm too fried to protest."

Andy said, "I've noticed something about you. You tend to have a lot of assumptions about people and a lot of assumptions about what people think of you. The only way to break those assumptions is to actually get to know them, and by that process allow them to get to know you."

"You sound like my mother."

He held up his hands. "You can lead a horse to water, but you can't make them drink."

"Okay Mr. Life Coach, at what point do we hold hands and dance to 'Kumbaya' off into the sunset?"

He smiled and shook his head. "I can't think of any other way to say it. Anyway, you're sick and we should probably talk about something else."

"No, you do have a point."

For the past three years, Andy had been like a brother to her. She felt like she could talk to him about anything – and she had. He'd sat through countless hours of her blabbing about everything from her family to her academics to her social life. And through it all, he would nod along and give advice when he deemed it necessary. She wasn't the only person he did this with. Everyone in their circle of friends expected him to go into psychiatry one day.

The problem was that his input lacked one thing: he didn't understand why she didn't put herself out there more. Interaction was a skill that had never come naturally to her. It had taken her until university to feel like she was an accepted member of a friend group. When she'd tried to open up to people in high school, it only exposed her awkwardness and made her an easy target for mockery.

Now, she was happy with the group of friends she had and she'd rather hang out with them or stay in her room and read. If someone asked her if she could live the rest of her life in a private paradise, away from the complexities and bullshit of day-to-day life, she would've told them her answer in a heartbeat.

"You know," she said, looking around. "I think Sans has the right idea."

"About what? Patio design?"

"No, about his lifestyle."

"The backyard isn't too shabby, I'll give him that," he said, gesturing out to the savanna.

"But I mean, he doesn't have to put up with so much of the crap we do. He talks on a video camera with people halfway around the world for several hours, works in his office just like he would have to in a city or anywhere else, but they can't touch him out here. He has amazing facilities and the opportunity to do what he loves all the time. I mean, why do you think he never leaves?"

Andy frowned. "I don't know. I definitely enjoy a good vacation once in a while, but if you don't go through the real world most of the time, how can you truly appreciate what it means to get away from it all? I mean, you can't call it a retreat if you have nothing to retreat from."

"Then you call it home," she said.

He looked at her. "We all need to get out of the house from time to time. Otherwise you'll go mad from cabin fever."

She thought for a moment and decided to change the subject. "So, what do you do with the data analysis again?"

"We review the information the implants send us to monitor and map the species' movement patterns. It's interesting, Sans has these little emitters in the ground around the perimeters of the reserve and if anything gets near them, the implant will zap them. Keeps his cloned creatures away from the rest of the lot without having to build a fence. He said this was less disruptive to the environment."

"But can't other animals still wander in?" she asked.

"I guess, but he didn't mention it being an issue."

"We saw something weird yesterday during our tagging op. There were all these wildebeest mauled and eaten, spread out over a short area. It didn't seem like any animal behavior I'd ever heard of before. Ramsay told us it must've been lions and didn't seem too concerned about it."

"That doesn't sound like normal lions."

The images of the gory scene came flooding back to her mind. The blood on the grass, the entrails all over the ground, the rotting stench of–

"Wait a minute," she said. "Could there have been a pathogen in the carcasses? One that could have been transmitted through the air, maybe?"

"I'm not sure I follow you. Why would the wildebeest have had a virus?"

"What if that's how I got sick? It's the only unusual thing I came into contact with yesterday. The killings don't match any normal animal behavior. So, what if some lions or something got infected with a weird new strain of a virus, like rabies."

"Now you think you have rabies?" Andy said, raising an eyebrow.

"No, not exactly, but... What if a group of infected animals killed those wildebeest? It explains the unusual circumstances and the lion-like imprints we found at the scene."

"It doesn't explain why you're not frothing at the mouth and trying to eat my face off."

"Okay, so maybe it's not rabies."

"And that doesn't make sense how it would be transmitted through the air."

Sydney thought for a moment, trying to remember if she'd accidentally touched something yesterday. *No*, she realized, *I didn't get within five feet of the bodies*. Then it hit her.

"The flies! There were flies buzzing around. I think one of them bit me." It would also explain why Ramsay wasn't showing any symptoms: he'd gone back to the car first and might not have been bitten. She'd have to see if Brandon was truly fighting something off or if there was another explanation for his sudden change in behavior. He had been near the carcasses for longer too.

"Most viruses don't jump species," Andy said.

"Rabies does."

"We just agreed this wasn't rabies."

"Maybe it's something similar. Or maybe it can't fully cross species but in humans it causes a fever and muscle soreness for a few days, and in lions it makes them—"

"Commit mass murder?"

She shrugged. "The animal equivalent."

Andy sighed. "Sydney, this is all very fun but I think there's a simpler explanation for all this."

"And that is?"

"You're just experiencing a side-effect of the vaccines. They affect everyone differently. Keep relaxing, get a good night's sleep, and you'll probably feel better tomorrow. If not, then surely in a few days."

"But what about the dead wildebeest?" she said.

"I don't know, but if Ramsay doesn't seem worried about it than I wouldn't be either."

She leaned back in her chair. "I guess not."

"Nature is a strange thing. Just when we think we have it nailed down, some outlier data throws everything off. We can make generalizations about animal behavior, but just like people, there are going to be rogues and exceptions."

She looked out at the shimmering heat off in the prairies and said nothing, knowing he was right.

She was given more aspirin around four and by dinner, she had enough of an appetite to eat a hamburger. After that, she'd actually felt she had the mental capacity to read again and spent a few hours in the library. Satisfied, she returned to her room around ten.

Nurse Graves had checked her out again after she was finished eating and gave her two more pills to take before bed. Sydney's fever was holding around a hundred now, which wasn't great, but compared to earlier felt lightyears better.

Closing the door behind her, she placed the pills and the book on her nightstand and was about to start brushing her teeth when something out the north-facing window caught her attention. She walked over and peered into the night.

Sydney could see the lights of two Land Rovers driving off into the reserve. She watched them until they gradually faded into the blackness.

It brought back a memory from the first day. Ramsay had been concerned about getting back before the sun went down for some reason and he hadn't even gotten worried about the strange attack on the wildebeest.

Something didn't quite add up but she felt much too tired to think about it. Instead, she looked out the other window towards the lights of the laboratory, which were still on. Then she witnessed something else.

Down on the ground below her, a figure dressed entirely in black moved towards the treeline. As they crouched and turned back to see if they were being spotted, she caught a glimpse of their face.

It was Jones.

"What the hell are you doing?" she muttered.

Sydney watched as he continued into the treeline and was swallowed up by the night.

She shook her head. Had she really seen that? It didn't look like he was just out for an evening stroll. She'd have to tell Andy about it in the morning.

Then her fever started to come back, her head heating up once more. She grabbed the pills off her nightstand, tossed them in her mouth, and washed them down with some water from the bottle Ramsay had given her the day before.

She brushed her teeth quickly and got into bed without pulling the sheets over her body. She didn't want to burn up.

Then, finally, she drifted off to sleep.

CAVE

Walking further into the endless dark, Richard Jones briefly turned on his flashlight to make sure he was headed in the right direction, then clicked it off again. He was moving along the edge of the trees, the lights of the laboratory off to his left. His eyes had adjusted as much as they could to the blackness, but the sliver of a moon wasn't providing much support and the flashlight would draw attention to him if he used it for too long.

He knew that Sans had electromagnetic emitters in a perimeter around the lodge, airstrip, and laboratory to prevent the animals from coming near, otherwise he would have been more worried. Still, he wasn't entirely sure if where he was going was inside the safe zone. It made him wish he had his old Glock with him, but he hadn't thought to bring it on the trip. Of course, he hadn't expected to be in this predicament.

He'd tried to make Chang see things his way, he really had, but she was too much of a believer in Billy Sans. Something wasn't right here and with the amount of money at stake, he couldn't stand by without knowing. He needed to get into that building.

The schematics he'd seen showed another entrance to the laboratory, one a few thousand feet away from the structure itself. He didn't get why Sans needed some secret passage or tunnel, but then again, he didn't get many things about that man. It was a fool's errand to think he could run the company from out here forever. It'd clearly made him think he was untouchable.

That night, as he hiked through the humid gloom, swatting mosquitoes away from his face, Jones was determined to correct that assumption.

He was currently clad in a black turtleneck, dark jeans, and a rugged pair of boots. As soon as Sans and Ramsay had gone out into the reserve for whatever reason, he'd slipped downstairs to the library without anyone seeing him and exited through the back doors. There was no alarm system to sound off a beeping noise through the lodge when he did so; after all, why would Sans need an alarm system in the middle of the African wilderness? Then he'd slipped away along the edge of the forest, reasonably sure he hadn't been seen.

The lights were on off in the distance of the veterinary labs. *What the hell are people still doing there at this hour?* he thought. Jones supposed he'd know soon enough. He didn't know how far he'd get, but he just wanted to catch a glimpse. It was his right to, after all. The employees here all worked for SansCorp, which meant they worked for him. And if anyone caught him, that's exactly what he'd tell them.

He clicked on his flashlight again, aiming the beam up ahead. The trees had ended and he was now wading through the grassland beneath the starry sky. It was amazing how much of the galaxy you could see with the naked eye when you had no light pollution. His thoughts returned to the task at hand. A rock formation jutted up a hundred feet away or so at the top of a small hill.

Jones swung the light around him, making sure he was still alone. No people or predators were in sight and there was no sound other than the soft symphony of the insects. He knew the emitters were roughly the size of lawn sprinklers, too small to look for at this hour unless you happened to accidentally trip over one. But he was certain Sans would have them extend past this second entrance; it wouldn't make sense to have it unprotected.

Still, there was a persistent sense of trepidation that gripped him as he finally reached the formation. Perhaps it was just all that he didn't know, starting several months ago when the strange expenditures had really begun to catch his attention. Perhaps it was the calm, measured way Sans had assured him and Chang that the project would pay off with the precision of a rehearsed performance. The whole thing had felt forced. Nothing added up.

Jones swung around the corner of the rocks and found himself staring into the black mouth of the cave. He shined the flashlight around the frame; it was about ten feet tall and fifteen feet wide. He swept the beam across the ground inside. The gray rock had been smoothed with time and dirt lay scattered around the entrance in almost trail-like formations, as if somebody had been in and out recently.

He inched forward and the cave engulfed him. The ground became more craggy and uneven as it sloped downward, requiring him to maintain the light on the floor before each footstep. *Why the hell would Sans use this? It must be a bitch trying to bring anything through here.*

Jones knew Sans didn't release animals brought in for care this way; they were driven back out into the prairies and let loose as they started to regain consciousness. This cave was clearly a natural construct; maybe Sans had built an emergency exit for the lab here since it was already next to where he was building. Of all the fire escapes in the world, this one didn't seem like the most direct or safest to climb out of, but he supposed it beat burning to death.

The tunnel widened into a more open space. There was the faint dripping of water from somewhere within the cavern and Jones shone his light towards the ceiling to see stalactites dangling above him like pointed daggers.

"Richard, what the hell are you getting yourself into?" he muttered.

The ground was much more level here, but he had to be careful of an edge about ten feet ahead of him. Getting closer, he could see it overlooked a roughly five-foot drop that led into the rest of the cave system, which appeared to be heading deeper. Suddenly, his right boot stepped on something and there was a soft crunch. He lifted his foot and aimed the flashlight downwards.

It was a bone. It looked worn, gnawed on, and it was caked in dried blood.

Shining the beam in a circle around him, he realized there were several others scattered all over the floor. And along the walls were more complete skeletons clumped in piles of animal skulls and shattered vertebrae. As his heart began to pound faster, Jones suddenly realized where he was.

A predator's den.

He backed up, beads of sweat rolling down his face. His throat tightened. That didn't make sense. Why would Sans have an underground door that backed into an animal's territory? Had the emitters malfunctioned around this area and allowed some of them to get in or–

The ground gave way behind him and he fell backwards, turning around in midair and twisting his right ankle. The flashlight tumbled off into the dark as he landed chest-first on the hard rock five feet down, the impact driving the breath out of his lungs.

Jones gasped, inadvertently inhaling some dust on the ground. He turned over and lurched upright, coughing. His ankle hurt like hell.

The noise echoed throughout the cavern.

He glanced around in the pitch blackness. The dripping sounded louder now, but he couldn't pinpoint its source. The flashlight was about ten feet behind him, leaning against a small boulder and shining at an angle deeper into the cave.

"Christ," he muttered, getting on his hands and knees. He was pretty sure he'd just sprained his ankle or at least hurt it pretty badly, so he began crawling towards the shining beacon.

Fuck, this was a bad idea, he thought. *Fuck the board, they're not worth this shit.*

Then a sound reached his ears and he froze.

Coming from back the way he came was the unmistakable growl of an animal, low and rumbling like a snarling dog. It grew louder for a second, then ceased entirely.

Oh Jesus, Jones thought, holding perfectly still. Goosebumps ran along his arms and every hair on his body felt on end. Where had that come from? He knew sound traveled farther in the cave. It had had a certain echoing quality to it, as if the animal was still back near the entrance.

He scurried forward towards the flashlight, expecting to hear a closer growl at any second. Instead there only the dripping of water, which was really starting to get on his nerves.

Jones finally reached the beam, grabbed it, and turned around, shining it back past the edge into the main cavern. He glimpsed a shadow dart away from the beam, gliding through the dark like a wraith. It was gone in a flash.

Whatever it was, it was huge. It had to be at least the size of a lion.

Maybe even bigger.

But he had seemingly scared it off. *Stupid animal*, he thought. *Scared of a fucking flashlight*. He allowed himself to laugh a little, just a light chuckle. It made him feel better. His death grip around the flashlight loosened slightly as he began to stand up, being careful to only put pressure on his left foot. His right ankle was still throbbing, but it probably wasn't sprained. He could limp back to the lodge, he'd just have to climb back up the ledge and then get out of this goddamn cave. He brought the flashlight back up–

And the thing was *right fucking there*, perched on the ledge and ready to spring.

Jones only had time to briefly register the ugly head with its horrifyingly sharp teeth and gleaming red eyes before the beast leapt. It collided with him in mid-air and he felt his body fly back several feet before crashing onto the rock floor, several of his ribs breaking as the creature pressed its entire weight into him.

He lifted his head and opened his mouth to scream when the thing swiped at him out of the darkness. Its claws hooked under the left hinge of his jawbone and the entire lower half of his mouth was ripped free.

Somehow, he didn't black out immediately from the pain. His eyes bulged out of his head, staring up at the monster as blood clogged his throat and spilled out onto the cave floor. The predator's red eyes came down towards him through the black. Jones felt hot breath on what was left of his face just before the animal wrapped its jaws around his cranium. Its bite pressure was immense and he felt its fangs piercing through flesh and bone. The agony seemed like it would never end–

Then, with a final hideous *crack*, his skull imploded.

PART II

PREY

DEPARTURE

She walked through the savanna beneath a crimson sky. The blood-red sun was perched on the horizon dead ahead of her, unmoving next to the silhouette of an acacia tree in the distance. A sense of fear slowly seeped through her body, but she was utterly transfixed by the glowing ball before her. It was as if it was pulling her closer by way of some magnetic force.

Abruptly, she felt the sensation of being watched and stopped dead in her tracks. She turned in a circle, glancing at the surrounding empty plains with a growing sense of dread. Some fifty feet off to her right, a shadow crouched in the grass. She stared at it for a moment, squinting to try and make out any defining features.

A pair of red eyes stared back at her. Then the shadow began to close in, moving like a lion.

Turning on her heel, she sprinted full force towards the sun. The red ball was sinking now, and disappearing fast. Despite her speed, the distant tree came no closer, fixed in the far-off reaches of the grassland. The sun vanished and the red sky dimmed to an overwhelming black.

She felt the shadow right behind her–

Sydney bolted awake to find herself drenched in sweat. She put a hand to her forehead and found it was cooler than yesterday, but still warm. Her fever must've broken. It made her want to feel relieved, but she was still aching all over. It was as if every part of her, inside and out, was recovering from a massive workout. Groaning, she got out of bed and headed towards the bathroom. Her belly rumbled loudly and she was at least glad that her appetite seemed to be returning.

She stopped and looked at herself in the mirror. There were bags under her eyes and she looked pale and tired, which echoed how she felt. Sydney took a moment to assess herself. At five-foot-eleven, she'd always been tall. It was one of the reasons her mother had insisted she play volleyball in high school; besides, she had said, being on the team would help her make friends. At first, she hadn't wanted to but some of her best friends back then came from the team, especially once they realized Sydney was a good player. It was why she had continued the sport at Georgetown. That, and it motivated her to stay fit.

Grabbing the pill bottle, she took out a primaquine tablet and tossed it onto her tongue. Then she filled the empty glass next to the faucet with water and took a large gulp. *All these fucking shots and meds and I still catch something,* she thought, feeling it slide down her throat. Even her esophagus felt achy.

She tried to take her mind off the discomfort as she completed her morning routine of brushing her teeth, showering, and getting dressed. Afterwards, she slowly made her way downstairs and entered the dining room. A few other people were already there.

Brandon was hunched over his French toast and bacon, looking like shit. His eyes also had bags beneath them and it seemed he could fall asleep and faceplant onto his food at any moment. *He is sick after all*, Sydney noted. At least now she knew this had something to do with the carrion of the wildebeest. Before she could figure out what though, she needed some breakfast. She was starving.

She sat down across from Andy; Courtney hadn't arrived yet. As usual, Sans was at the head of the table reading something on an iPad next to his plate. Chang was by his side, but Jones was nowhere to be seen. She was wondering what he'd been up to the night before when a servant saw she had arrived through the open kitchen door and brought her some slices of French toast with a side of potato hash. She quickly dug in and polished everything off in a couple minutes.

The server came back out a moment later to collect Andy's plate and saw she had finished. "Would you like some more?" he asked.

"Yes, please," she said, rubbing her stomach.

Andy raised an eyebrow. "Feeling better?"

"A little," she said. A burp escaped her lips and she covered her mouth in embarrassment.

Andy shook his head. "Always a shining model of elegance."

Just then, Courtney stormed into the room and slammed both of her palms down on the table. Her eyes stared dead ahead toward Sans.

"I need to leave."

Sans looks baffled. "I don't understand."

"I need to go home."

"Why?"

"It's an emergency!"

"It must not be a family emergency," Sans said. "You've had no contact with your family since getting here. You signed a non-disclosure agreement. We can't risk a data breach."

She squeezed her eyes shut and breathed deeply, then regained her composure. "It's a personal emergency. I can't take being here anymore. I need to leave. Now. Today. You can't hold me here against my will."

"Courtney, look around," he said. "No one here is holding you against your will. However, the next supply flight isn't until Monday and it's only Thursday. Besides, your commercial flight from Nairobi doesn't leave until next Sunday."

"Reschedule it. I forsake the internship, I forsake any recommendation letters, everything. Just get me out of here." She looked frazzled, her finger nails digging into the wood.

Sans sat still, gears clearly turning in his mind. He finally said, "I'll see what I can do."

"Thank you," Courtney said, relieved. She turned back into the foyer and disappeared up the stairs.

Sydney was baffled. What did she think she was doing? This internship was the opportunity of a lifetime and she was throwing it away.

The servant came out with Sydney's seconds a moment later. As she ate, she glanced over at Sans. He looked deep in thought as he scratched his chin. Chang looked perplexed as she continued with her breakfast, but ultimately remained silent.

Since both Brandon and Sydney weren't feeling well, Ramsay decided to give them the day off. She went to the library and finished the Crichton novel, which gave her time to flip through some of the Capstick books.

She was reading a chapter on leopards in *Death in the Long Grass* when Andy walked in.

"I told her not to do it."

Sydney looked up. "What do you mean?"

"I told her not to leave. She insisted she had to go," he said, taking a seat. "We talked a fair bit over the past few days. She liked it here at first, but then she started getting weirded out by things."

"Like what?"

"She was just getting paranoid about dumb shit, like why the lab basement was off limits. I told her that's probably where they worked on some of the company's more high-level projects. Things that would be, as they say, 'above our paygrade'."

"That's why she left?"

"She questioned other things too. She thought it was weird that Sans never left the reserve and… I don't know. I think she was mostly homesick."

"Couldn't handle being away from her phone, probably," Sydney smirked.

Andy frowned. "I'm not sure. I think there was more that she just wasn't telling me. The vibe, she said…the vibe of this place is wrong."

"What's she talking about? This place is amazing. If I weren't sick, I'd be enjoying this week much more."

"She tried to convince me to leave with her, and to convince you too since I know you. She said she tried to talk to Brandon about it yesterday evening, but he was being a dick."

"And what did you say?"

"I just told her she could do whatever she wanted, but that I was staying and I knew you'd do the same."

"Damn right, I am. If that idiot wants to torpedo her grad school chances, she's not dragging us down with her."

Ramsay entered the room.

"Lunch is ready," he announced.

Sans was once again sitting at the head of the table. Plates were prepared with sandwiches and he waited until they were seated to speak. "We're just waiting on Brandon," he said. "He'll be here momentarily."

A few seconds later, Brandon was led into the room by Graves, who looked cold and detached as usual. Once he was in his chair, Sans resumed talking.

"Courtney left about an hour ago on the plane. She's being flown to Nairobi as we speak, where she'll board a flight for Amsterdam that connects to New York later this evening. Fortunately, we were able to get this all arranged even at the very last minute. It turned out that, due to an emergency, someone on the Amsterdam flight had cancelled a few hours ago and that they were booked all the way back to the States." Sans shrugged. "Sometimes, things just line up. Regardless, I'm not sure why she chose to leave four days in, but that is her choice. I hope that if any of you have comments or concerns, you will direct to them to me. I'd like to remind you that I personally selected you from a large pool of candidates and I value your input deeply. Just let me know." He smiled.

They all nodded.

"Good. I know Sydney, Brandon, you two have been feeling under the weather lately. Nurse Graves will continue to monitor you and I hope you recover soon. With luck, next week will run much smoother."

He stood up and made his way for the foyer just as Chang walked in. "Have you seen Jones?" Sydney heard her ask.

"I'm sorry, I haven't," Sans said. "He must be around."

He continued on as Chang, looking concerned, joined them at the table for lunch. Sydney thought about when she had last seen Jones, dressed in all black and sneaking away into the dark. Her mind mulled over that image as she ate her sandwich.

That night around ten o'clock, Sydney was finishing brushing her teeth when she saw distant, moving lights out of the north-facing window. She spat the toothpaste into the sink and walked over to get a better view.

Just like the night before, there were two Land Rovers driving off into the savanna. She went to the western window and watched the ground for the next several minutes, half-expecting to see Jones slinking off again. She didn't. In fact, she hadn't seen the man all day. Chang's face had been a mixture of worry and confusion at dinner. She'd barely paid attention as Sans narrated the story of a near-death brush with a lion in South Africa. And then there was what Andy had said about Courtney not telling him everything.

Things weren't adding up. Something wasn't right here.

Sydney decided to put those thoughts out of her mind and went to sleep.

CAUSE FOR CONCERN

The next morning was Friday. Sydney entered the dining room to find that Brandon wasn't there. It was strange, she thought, given that he had been here before her every day this week. Andy sat at his usual place while Sans and Chang were situated at the head of the table, but there was still no sign of Jones.

She sat down across from Andy and began devouring the omelet in front of her. Sydney felt just as hungry as she had yesterday, but now it felt as if the fever was starting to come back. She'd almost gotten used to the dull ache that seemed to permeate every fiber of her body. At least her stomach would feel better once it had food in it.

Sydney wondered if she should ask Ramsay for another day off. With Courtney bailing out, her work ethic would still look good by comparison. And it wasn't like she was slacking; she'd been feeling sick for the past three days now. She thought about the flies swirling around the decaying carcasses. Had that really been the cause of all this? Or was it something simpler, like Andy had said? Just a nasty side effect of the vaccines?

She wanted to see if there had been any other strange animal kills in the past few days, and she wanted to have tests run on the dead wildebeest, if there was anything still left of them at this point.

A moment later, Ramsay led Graves in through the front door and straight up the stairs towards the bedrooms.

"I guess Brandon's taking a sick day," Andy said, sipping orange juice. "If he can't make it, would you mind if I joined you out in the field?"

"Sure," Sydney said, her mood brightening. "Is that allowed?"

Andy shrugged. "I don't have a partner anymore, so I'm sure Ramsay wouldn't mind if I 'tagged along' for the day." He winked.

She put a hand to her head. "Fuck off."

Ramsay said he'd have to ask Sans for approval, but a few minutes later he came back and told them yes. They both got dressed into safari gear and met in the garage, where Ramsay went over the injector procedure with Andy. Then they drove out into the reserve.

"What's the difference between the Mark VIIs and the Mark VIs?" Andy asked.

"Mark VII monitors vital signs," Ramsay said, keeping focused on the terrain ahead.

An idea suddenly popped into Sydney's head. "So it would tell you if the animals are dead or not?"

"That is correct."

"And it tells you from the GPS, right?"

"Yes, the Mark VII-chipped animals will have their dot on the map change to gray if the device stops reading vital signs."

"Have any of them died since we've tagged them?" Sydney asked.

"We've only tagged 14 this week, but–"

"Can we zoom out on the whole reserve?" she asked, leaning forward.

"Give me a moment," Ramsay said, alternating between looking ahead and tapping the touchscreen to adjust the viewing area. She saw red dots all over the map for the animals with only Mark VIs, but the ones with the latest implants had both red and blue dots side by side since both iterations of the chip were still active. In an area towards the border with Serengeti National Park, there was a lone, unmoving animal with both a red and a gray dot overlapping. "One of them is deceased," he said, then frowned. "That's odd."

"What is it?" Andy asked.

Ramsay turned the wheel to steer them in a new direction. "It's an elephant."

The Land Rover slowed down at the top of a small hill. Below, a river ten feet across twisted through the land. All three of them climbed out of the vehicle and walked forward to get a better look. Sydney felt her hairs stand on end as she gazed down at the sight before her.

Resting on the riverbank was an enormous, bloodied skeleton. Large chunks of flesh still clung to the bone in some places, and the ribcage was shattered. Pieces of it lay on the ground near scattered remnants of the creature's intestinal tract. The head was intact, but the eyes had been eaten and there wasn't much meat left on the skull. The two ivory tusks, however, were unscathed.

"Well at least we know it wasn't poachers," Andy remarked.

Ramsay squatted and examined the ground nearby. A moment later, he stood up. "Hyenas have been here."

"But what *killed* it?" Sydney asked, growing worried. "Adult elephants have no natural predators. They're too big."

"It could've been injured," Ramsay said. "Weak animals are always susceptible to attack."

She shielded her eyes with her hand and squinted down at the remains, carefully scanning the entire body for any sign of a fracture that wasn't clearly caused by the attack. "The legs are all fine. The damage to the ribcage must've been from the killers."

"Maybe it was sick," Ramsay shot back. "Whatever the reason was, something killed this animal. My guess is a pride of lions. But now it is dead, and there is nothing we can do about it. That's how nature works." He started walking back to the driver's side door.

Sydney followed him. "Wait, but that's not normal. There have been two instances of strange predatory behavior here over the past week, starting with the wildebeest. And I bet there's more. Look for more small dot clusters of herbivores that aren't moving. Look for unusual migration patterns within the limits of the reserve."

Ramsay turned around and folded his arms. "What are you getting at? Sans personally selected which animals at which zoos he wanted DNA taken from to create a perfectly stable ecosystem. They were all healthy and normal. We have a complete list of species here and keep a close watch on all of them. There are no surprises here."

"Then how do you explain that?" Andy chimed in.

Ramsay's eyes narrowed. "I told you. It probably got sick."

"But when we tagged it a few days ago it was perfectly fine," Sydney said, remembering.

"It *seemed* fine. Viruses can lay low within a host's body. Sometimes the primary symptoms don't come out until days or weeks after it has entered an animal's system. The early effects might be mild or not even noticed at all. We saw this elephant for no more than fifteen minutes."

"The animals can't get out of the reserve because of the electromagnetic emitters, right?" she asked.

Ramsay nodded. "That is correct."

"But what about something else getting in?"

"What do you mean?"

Sydney wiped sweat from her brow. "I think there might be an invasive species here, or a species infected with some behavior-altering virus. And I think the virus was left in those carcasses earlier in the week, and the flies transmitted it to both me and Brandon by biting us."

Ramsay looked as if he was trying hard not to laugh. "I don't think that's what's going on here."

"But it makes sense. You were probably right about the lions – but they've been infected with something, kind of like a rabies virus – but not rabies, obviously, cause Brandon and I don't have rabies and…" She realized she was starting to ramble now and making herself look like an idiot.

"There's a rational explanation for all of this," Ramsay said. "I'm sure your sickness is related to the vaccines and in a few days, will be a distant memory. This" – he pointed to the elephant carcass – "is the result of predators preying upon a weakened animal. And I'm sure there's a good explanation for the wildebeest too. Just because we don't know it yet doesn't mean we should jump to conclusions."

He opened the door. "Now, we have work to do."

Sydney headed for the back. Andy continued to stare

down at the skeleton for a moment, then he followed her.

"There's definitely something going on out there," Andy said. They were sitting on the second-story balcony, sipping some pina coladas that Fatou had made them. Sydney figured if she could have several more of these, she actually might start to feel better.

"Do you think Courtney was maybe right to leave?" she asked.

"What do you mean? Of course not. You're not thinking of–"

"No, no," she said. "It's just…don't you find it weird that Ramsay doesn't want to consider any other possibilities?"

"No, not really. He's the type of person who doesn't like to draw conclusions prematurely. I don't blame him. Personally, I'd say something is unusual with that dead elephant and the other animals you described earlier this week. But I'm sure there's a reason that makes sense. We just haven't found it."

"But what about everything else going on here?"

"Like what?"

"Like Jones."

"What about him?"

"Haven't you noticed he's been suspiciously absent these past two days?"

"He's got to be around here somewhere Sydney," Andy said. "We're in the middle of the Serengeti. Where could he have gone?"

"A few nights ago, I saw him sneaking around outside my window. He went off into the woods and the next day he'd disappeared. Doesn't that seem suspicious?"

Andy massaged his forehead. "You've been reading too many Crichton novels."

"And on the first day, Ramsay was all worried about us

not getting back before dark. But for the past two nights, I've seen these Land Rovers driving out there." She pointed to the grasslands. "And on top of that, we've got something eating fully-grown elephants that nobody seems to care about. I mean, for fuck's sake, how are you not worried about this?"

Andy took a deep breath. "I'll admit, it's all a little strange."

"Just a little?"

"Maybe more than a little, but Sans knows what he's doing. If there was something *really* wrong out there, he'd do something about it."

Her eyes lit up. "What if he already is?"

"I don't follow."

"What if they're heading out each night to try and track down the predators or whatever is doing this? I mean, predators hunt at night."

"And why wouldn't they tell us?" Andy said. "We've signed NDAs."

"What if they didn't want us to be worried about working out there?" Sydney said. "Or they don't know enough yet to want to tell us."

"Well, there's no way for us to find out."

"We could sneak into the garage and attach a camera to one of the Land Rovers and see where they go…"

Andy shook his head. "This isn't a Tom Cruise movie, Syd."

"But come on, we've done stuff like this before. I mean, remember that frat party where we had to sneak upstairs to get Megan's stolen phone back? I had to leave through the fire escape."

"And for the record, I advised against that."

"They always leave around ten at night. We could do it around nine and review the footage tomorrow."

"Do you have a camera?" he asked.

"I brought a GoPro for safaris and stuff but I haven't used it because I'm not sure how strict they are with the NDA. We're not allowed to take photos of the lab equipment, but I'm not sure if filming the savanna at night counts."

"I'm pretty sure spying on them would be a direct violation."

"Come on, we can do it," she said.

"Wouldn't the battery die before they get out there?"

"It has enough for two hours. If we put it on just after nine and they leave at ten, we'll have at least the first hour of whatever they do."

"Does it have a night mode?"

"No, but if we put it right under the mounted lights, we'll see enough," she affirmed.

"And how do you know which Rovers they'll take out?"

"We've only ever used the first two closest to the door during the day and I think I saw some extra equipment on the ones at the far end."

He sighed and looked off the balcony.

"Please," she said. "And then if it's a bunch of nothing, you can mock me for this all next year."

"Alright," he said, hefting his pina colada. "But when this is done, I'm going to need another one of these."

GARAGE

Everything was pitch black outside the windows as they crept downstairs. Sydney stopped and peered forward, trying to see if anyone was sitting in the dining room. The coast was clear. They continued into the foyer and hung a right, moving down the corridor that led towards the garage. Another hallway branched off here for the staff living quarters, so they waited a moment and listened for sounds before proceeding.

Finally, they reached the door.

Sydney glanced behind them to make sure no was coming, then she and Andy entered and gently closed the door behind them so it wouldn't swing shut. She glanced around. It was dark, the only light coming from a tiny fluorescent strip hanging from the center of the room. She could barely make out the vehicles as shadowy shapes in the faint glow. Andy reached for the light switch.

"Don't," she said.

"Why not?"

"If anyone comes in and sees the lights on, we're toast."

"Are there flashlights?"

"Check around."

Feeling along the wall beside her, she found what felt like a rope.

"Got some, over here," Andy said from a few feet away. He clicked on a large LED flashlight, illuminating a table before him that had several more waiting next to a load of other night gear. Sydney grabbed one and turned it on, shining the powerful beam around the room. She felt goosebumps on her skin and the feeling that they shouldn't be in here.

"Let's do this quickly," she said.

"It was your idea."

"I know, but we can still get it done quickly."

She slid past the front grill of the first Rover and started making her way down the row. Sure enough, as she shone the beam across the two vehicles at the far end, she saw they'd been retrofitted with additional racks.

"Can you find some tape?" she said.

She could see Andy's light dancing around on the shelves at the back of the garage. "I'm looking."

Sydney glanced at her watch. 9:05. Sans most likely wasn't going to leave for another hour, but she didn't know at what point he and his staff came in here to set up.

"Found some," Andy said, pulling a roll of duct tape off a rack—

And accidentally knocking over a toolbox, which opened upon impact and spilled its contents all over the floor. The metal tools clattered loudly as they tumbled to a halt.

"Shit," Sydney hissed, rushing over.

Andy was frantically trying to put the hammer, screwdrivers, and scattered screws back in the box. She crouched down and helped him. "Can you hear anyone coming?" he asked.

She stood up for a moment and listened towards the door. Nothing. She got back down on her knees and started picking up screws. "Not yet, but just hurry."

They managed to get everything into the container, shut it, and put it back on the shelf.

That was when the door opened.

Both of their flashlights went off almost immediately and Sydney blindly stumbled over to the rear of the closest SUV. She felt Andy behind her a moment later.

"Hello? Is anyone in there?" a South African accent called out.

She focused on keeping slow, quiet deep breaths. *There's nothing here. Just shut the door and go away–*

The lights came on.

Sydney could hear the man walking around to look behind the cars. He stopped. She gulped, her fingers tightening around her flashlight.

Then she heard footsteps receding. The room went dark again and the door closed.

She and Andy spent another minute remaining still, then Sydney stood up and turned on her beam. She turned towards the last Land Rover. "Let's do this one," she whispered.

She opened the driver's door, which automatically activated some interior lights, and stood on the floor in front of the seat as she inspected the light rigs and took the GoPro out of her pocket. She could hear Andy fumbling with the tape in the dark behind her. Finally, he handed her a strip.

"Can you hold my flashlight?" she asked.

He took hers and placed it down on the ground, then handed her the tape and shone his beam where she was working.

She pressed the camera into the bar and began applying the strip. Afterwards, she held out her hand for another.

"Hold on," he said. The light shone away from her and towards the ground as he tore off another long piece. "Here you go."

"Do you think we could get some food after this? I'm feeling hungry again."

"Sure, I'll call up UberEats and ask them if they do air delivery."

She rolled her eyes, rubbing the wrinkles out of the tape on top of the camera. "Come on, isn't there a pantry with snacks in it or something?"

"I think there might be one in the kitchen. Can we please stay focused?"

She held out her hand. "Tape," she said. He sighed and fumbled with the roll again. Two strips later, she patted the last of the adhesive into place and switched the device on. "There."

"Done?"

"Yeah, let's get out of here." She jumped down and closed the car door, then scooped her flashlight off the floor.

Quietly, they made their way around the backs of the Rovers toward the exit, turned off the flashlights, and left them on the table. Sydney felt around in the dark for the handle and cautiously turned it down, pulling the door open as slightly as possible so that she could still see through the crack.

She looked out into the hallway. No one was visible and all was silent. She waited for a moment, just wanting to be sure. Then she said, "Coast's clear."

With Andy right behind her, she opened it wider and prepared to step into the hall. Just then, a figure came around the corner from the staff quarters. She immediately backed up, bumping into Andy, and closed the door over. A moment later, she took a peek.

A man wearing white medical technician's clothes was walking away from her into the foyer. She watched as he turned for the front door, which she saw open and close. Then he was gone. He must've been going to the laboratory building. She still didn't get what they were doing there at this hour.

"Is he gone?" Andy breathed into her ear.

She nodded and opened the door again. The pair of them stepped out and Andy softly pulled the door closed until he heard a soft *click* and sighed with relief. They then walked quickly toward the foyer. Sydney felt her shoulders relax and the tense feeling in her body receded to the usual soreness she'd been feeling for the past few days.

Ahead of them, Graves walked around the corner. She looked surprised and stopped in her tracks. "What are you two doing here?"

Sydney was caught off guard. She was about to stutter an answer, when mercifully Andy intervened.

"We're just walking around. We've been reading for the past few hours, just wanted to stretch our legs."

The nurse's cold eyes regarded each of them with suspicion. "Have a good evening," she said. It didn't sound like she meant it. She brushed past them and disappeared into the staff corridor.

Without further delay, Sydney and Andy walked briskly into the foyer and up the stairs.

"How will we get it tomorrow?" he asked as they approached their rooms.

"I'll grab it off the car after the tagging."

"Won't Ramsay see you?"

"I'll think of something."

"What if Sans doesn't go out tonight?" he asked.

She shrugged. "Then this was all for nothing. Good night." She opened her door, then looked behind her. "Oh, and

Andy?"

"Yes?"

"Thanks for helping out."

"Always, but you do know you're crazy, right?"

"Of course."

She shut the door and then flopped on the bed, glancing at the clock. It was 9:17 now. She still had forty minutes or more until they left. If they left at all, that was. Andy's words stung at the back of her mind. What if the last two nights were a fluke? What if they had just risked getting caught for nothing? She couldn't leave the camera up there all day. The battery would be long dead, so she'd have to take it down, charge it, and then put it up again tomorrow night if she wanted another chance.

She sighed and rubbed her forehead. The fever was coming back. She got up and went to her bathroom, where the container of extra-strength painkillers that Graves had given her this morning lay. She took her nightly two with water, then paced the room for several minutes. She looked at the clock.

9:24.

Sydney groaned and resolved to brush her teeth and get ready, since walking around wasn't doing anything for her. After she'd gotten into her pajamas, she checked the time again. 9:36. Closer.

She paced her room and kept coming back to the window, just in case Sans decided to leave early. But there was nothing out there. She looked off at the laboratory building, obscured by the trees. Its lights were on as usual. She glanced down at the ground. Still no sign of Jones.

Sydney repeated this in a cycle until the clock finally displayed 10:00. Chewing on a fingernail, she peered out the northern window again. Still nothing, granted the convoy hadn't left until a few minutes past the hour for the last couple nights.

But for the next half an hour, nothing came.

Her empty stomach kept grumbling irritably, but she knew she wouldn't have anything to eat until morning. Angrily, she went back to the window. "Where are you, you bastards?" she muttered.

There was nothing out there but an empty plain, barely visible beneath the starry night sky.

Fuck it. She turned off her lights and climbed into bed. Maybe Sans was going out later. Or maybe he really wasn't going out at all. Tomorrow, she'd have her answer.

CAMERA

Sydney carefully slid the injector's syringe into the zebra's neck and squeezed the trigger. There was the metallic *hiss* of pressurized air escaping as the implant went in. Relieved, she pulled the device away and wiped sweat from her brow.

"That's the last one," she said.

Ramsay was standing not far behind her with his arms crossed, a blank expression on his face. "Good," he said. "Congratulations, you've completed all your tagging assignments."

She stood up, still feeling sore. Her fever had also been getting worse throughout the morning, but not quite to the level it had been on Wednesday. At least, not yet.

"Shame Brandon couldn't be here," she said, glancing at the three zebras she'd just upgraded to Mark VIIs.

"He's still not feeling well, but Nurse Graves says he should be fine in a few days." Ramsay started leading her back to the car.

As she was about to climb into the passenger seat, she took one last look around at the savanna. She wasn't sure if Sans would let them do one final safari next Saturday, but regardless that was still a way's away. Next week, she'd be huddled up in the lab analyzing the data from the new implants and Andy would be out here. She wasn't sure if he would have to do the entire week without a partner, though. Courtney's departure had really thrown things off.

The vehicle began driving back to the lodge. Sydney let her arm hang out the window, feeling the cool air run between her fingers. She glanced over at Ramsay, who appeared detached and silent as usual, sitting upright as if someone was pulling a string from the top of his head. She wondered how he and Sans had met, what his history was before he came to a place like this. Had he been in the military or a militia? Was he a big-game hunter? He clearly knew the sport. She figured she didn't know how to broach the subject properly and dropped it from her mind.

Eventually, they made it back to the lodge and Ramsay turned the Rover around to reverse it into its spot in the garage, a retractable door opening behind them. The SUV rolled into place and Ramsay turned it off. They got out and went through the door into the interior of the lodge.

Sydney waited until they'd passed the hallway that led to the staff rooms, then said, just as she'd rehearsed in her mind since breakfast, "Oh crap, I think I left my water bottle in the car." In truth, she had.

Ramsay rolled his eyes. "Go get it."

"Thanks," she said, hurrying back into the garage and shutting the door behind her. The retractable door just finished closing as she flicked on the main lights and proceeded to the Land

Rover at the very end of the row.

Moving quickly, she threw open the door, stepped up onto the floormat, and gripped the upper racks with one hand as she looked closely beneath the lighting rig. The GoPro was still there, untouched from where she left it. She pried both it and the tape loose from the metal bar as fast as she could, not wanting Ramsay to wonder why she was taking so long to grab a bottle.

Sydney shoved the camera and tape into one of her shorts' pockets and retrieved her water bottle from where she'd left it under the seat of the car they'd just been in. She had purposely put it down there instead of the cup-holder so Ramsay wouldn't notice it getting left behind and blow her reason for coming back.

She was expecting him to make some remark about her lack of speed when she returned inside, but instead found he hadn't waited for her and was long gone. Even better. She walked up the stairs and, checking over her shoulder to make sure no one was around, knocked on Andy's door. He should've been back from the lab building by now.

Sure enough, he opened it. "Come on in," he said.

She stepped through the door and he closed it. His suitcase was set up on the floor, leaving the desk for his laptop. She'd given him her mini-USB adapter that morning and it sat hooked up to the computer, waiting.

"It might need to charge for a little bit," Sydney said, glancing outside at the afternoon sky as she plugged it in.

"That's fine. But what were you starting to say earlier? You're not sure if they went last night?"

She shook her head. "Not by the time I went to sleep."

"So this might be just two hours of a darkened garage?"

"Maybe."

Andy scratched the back of his head. "Well, we might be in for some riveting entertainment then."

Sydney sighed and opened up the camera files. Knowing

the two hours of footage would take up a lot of space, she'd moved everything off the SD card and onto her own computer. Therefore, this thing had had 32GB of space free to record whatever it needed, which should've been more than enough. There was only one video as she clicked open the DCIM folder. The details read:

0116.MP4   07/17/2020   11:27 PM   MP4 File   12 GB   02:12:14

So it had recorded nearly an hour after she'd gone to sleep. She hit the Enter key and pulled up the video in the default media player. At first it was just pitch blackness, which was to be expected. She clicked ahead at multiple points throughout the first hour just to make sure nothing changed, then clicked ahead past the one and a half hour mark. Still nothing.

Sydney began to grow worried as Andy came up behind her and leaned over her shoulder. "Anything?" he asked.

"Not yet." She kept clicking until she got to a point where there was just under half an hour left. She leaned back in the chair and crossed her arms over her chest. "This is hopeless."

Then the lights came on.

They both leaned forward. Only the garage door was displayed before them, brightly illuminated by the lighting rig above the camera. It stayed that way for several minutes.

"Good thing the Rovers are electric," Andy said. "Otherwise they'd all be dead of carbon monoxide by now."

Suddenly, the retractable door opened before them and the upper lights and headlamps pierced through the darkness outside. There was nothing to see yet, just the trail winding off into the blackness. Then, after another moment, the vehicle began to move forward.

"What if it's just driving for thirty minutes?" she wondered aloud.

"Then we're screwed."

She clicked ahead a couple of times more. Still more driving, although by now they were well out in the savanna. Finally, with ten minutes left of footage, the SUV rolled to a halt.

Sydney watched intently for any sign of movement, but there was none. The grass swayed gently in the night breeze. Faintly, she could hear the sound of a door slamming and upped the computer's volume. Someone was speaking, then another voice farther away. Ramsay walked in front of the car.

He squatted in full view of the headlights and appeared to be looking at something on the ground. It was exactly how he'd examined the dirt after discovering the wildebeest carcasses and the dead elephant.

"They're looking for prints," she said.

"They're certainly tracking something," Andy added.

On the screen, Ramsay stood up and shouted, "Over here!"

Then Sans walked into view, holding some kind of tranquilizer gun. He seemed to be suited in full safari gear. There was something resting on his forehead she couldn't make out. She watched him talk to Ramsay for a moment, then they disappeared on opposite sides of the car: Ramsay towards the driver's side door and Sans towards the passenger seat. Shortly after that, the car began driving again. It continued like that for the next six minutes and twenty-two seconds.

Then the battery died on the camera and the footage abruptly ended.

The two of them sat silently for a moment.

"Well," Andy eventually said, "you are right. They were tracking some type of animal out there."

"But what?" Sydney said. She kept turning over the video in her mind. Some detail hadn't seemed right, but she was trying to place it. "Wait, go back to when they're standing in front of the car."

Andy rewound the video to Ramsay crouching.

"No, no," she said. "Keep going, until Sans walks in."

He dragged the bar a few short spaces forward and got to where Sans began to approach his assistant.

"There," she said. "Pause it right there."

Andy did so. "What is it?"

She didn't answer, her eyes focusing intently on the thing sitting atop Sans's head. She realized what it reminded her of: night vision goggles. Of course, that made sense with searching for animals in the dark. But something else seemed off. It was suggested first by the way Sans was dressing; he looked more prepared than for an average safari.

And that's when she realized: The weapon he was holding wasn't a tranquilizer at all.

It was a hunting rifle.

TROPHIES

Brandon was still nowhere to be seen at dinner, so she and Andy sat beside Chang and Ramsay that evening. It was grilled salmon, prepared with Fatou's "secret recipe" marinade, and Sydney tried not to wolf it down too quickly. The fever was getting much worse again but her appetite seemed to only be getting stronger. She hoped there was dessert.

"I'd just like to congratulate you again on completing your first week here," Sans said, looking between her and Andy. She saw that he was wearing the same Pathfinder watch, but now sported a blue sweatband around his other wrist. "You've both done excellent work."

"Thank you," Andy said.

She swallowed a bite and chimed in, "It's been wonderful."

"You'll switch positions on Monday. Hopefully Brandon will have recovered by then. As for your partner Andy, I'm still thinking of something. Perhaps Brandon can join you for a few days for tagging since he's missed some field work."

"That sounds good."

Sans looked at her. "Sydney, how are you feeling?"

"Better," she lied.

"Glad to hear it," Sans said. "I see you've been eating well."

She looked down and realized her plate was clean. "Oh...I..."

He smiled and put up a hand. "I'll tell Fatou his cooking is appreciated. Can I get you anything else? It's no inconvenience."

Normally, she would've politely declined. But she felt as if she'd barely eaten anything. "Could I have some more?" she asked.

"Absolutely. Fatou!" Sans called into the kitchen. "Could you have someone bring Sydney another plate?"

It was then she noticed Chang hadn't been following their conversation. She looked deep in thought, staring at the table as she fiddled with her fork.

A servant brought Sydney's second plate. As she thanked him and started eating, Sans looked around the table.

"I know it's felt strange these past few days," he said, seemingly to no one in particular. "With Courtney leaving and Brandon bedridden, our group has certainly felt...smaller. And it came to my attention that another guest, Mr. Richard Jones, has been failing to keep up appearances for the past few days. Well, now we know why."

Sydney froze just as she was about to take a bite and looked up. Everyone was focused on Sans except for Chang, but Ramsay looked as if he already knew.

"We found him last night, or at least, what was left of him." Sans took a deep breath, glancing at his wine glass. "He'd gone out into the reserve, presumably after dark. There's no clear reason why he would go out alone, but Richard was always one to stick his nose in other people's business." He took a sip, then sat silently drumming his fingers on the wood. "We often forget how dangerous nature really is. All these children's movies and stuffed animals try to make lions and leopards look so cuddly and harmless. So many conservationists develop a moral high ground where they believe these creatures are hopeless without their intervention, like they're gods coming down from ivory towers to save the day. They forget that these things don't need us. In fact, they're better off without us.

"I don't hunt to feel superior. I hunt to remind myself how fragile we really are. That despite all our advances, all of our progress, when I go out into the wild there's a great chance an animal guided solely by instinct will tear me apart and consume my flesh for energy. I remember that fact every time I set foot out there. Richard, clearly, did not. May he rest in peace."

Sans stood up, pushed in his chair, and walked out of the room with his wine glass in hand. After a moment, Ramsay followed him. Chang hadn't moved, still silently turning the fork over on her placemat again and again and again. Sydney put her utensils down.

Her appetite was gone.

As she climbed the stairs, the quietness of the lodge seemed unsettling. It was also dawning on her that she had been the last one to see Jones alive. The image of him vanishing into the forest replayed over and over again in her mind. For him to have been attacked, he must've gone outside the electromagnetic perimeter. But what was out there that would make him do something so stupid?

She and Andy returned to their respective rooms without saying a word. Sydney flopped onto her bed and lay on her back, staring at the wooden ceiling. She thought back to that conversation she'd overheard on Tuesday night, just Chang and Jones alone in the library. Jones had said Sans's latest project was using up more company funds than originally expected and he'd wanted to take a look around the veterinary labs. There was something about the interns not be allowed to see everything, and some kind of second entrance through a cave out in the reserve.

The cave. That's where he must've been heading that night. But before he could get there, something killed him. Sans had said they'd found "what was left of him", and Sydney tried to shut images of bloody human remains out of her mind. She hoped her imagination was worse than what had actually happened to him.

Something still didn't make sense. Was the cave entrance outside the perimeter? Why would Sans have an unguarded access point to his labs? Didn't that defeat the point, or was it a way of releasing animals from the lab directly into the wild? She wondered if the same creatures that had killed the wildebeest and the elephant had gotten Jones. Did that mean they were roaming right near the lodge?

Sydney stood up. Whenever she needed to clear her mind or think through something, she would often go for a walk. She left her room and went across the hall to knock on Andy's door.

He opened it. "What's up?"

"Wanna go for a stroll?"

"Outside? It's buggy as hell."

"I think Sans has mosquito-repellent candles on the pool deck," she said.

"Alright," he said, throwing on some shoes.

As they walked down the hall to the landing at the top of

the stairs, Andy turned and looked at the two double doors with the ferns on each side. "You know, I wonder what he keeps in there."

"It's his trophy room."

They turned to see Chang coming up the stairs. "It also doubles as his office and bedroom. He doesn't allow anyone in there, not even the staff. I talked to them about it. It's his inner sanctum, the one place he can go where no one can touch him. He wouldn't dare show me, and I've been his friend since grad school."

"You both went to Stanford, right?" Sydney asked.

"That's correct." She sighed and looked at the doors. There was a moment of silence, then she finally said, "He hasn't been the same since she died."

"Who?" Andy said.

"His wife, Jane. Only thing he loved more than her was probably hunting itself."

It struck Sydney as odd that Sans hadn't mentioned her before. And she hadn't seen any photos of her around the lodge. "She must've been into hunting too, then."

Chang shook her head and chuckled. "Actually no, she hated it. She was always a big eco-warrior, and I guess he is too, but Billy's always had this Darwinist grove about things." She smirked and drew a flask from her pocket. She took a swig and Sydney realized it probably hadn't been her first this evening.

"How'd they ever end up together?" Andy said, almost laughing.

Chang screwed the cap back on. "She saved him from killing himself."

Sydney and Andy were silent.

"What, you thought those colorful sweatbands were some kind of fashion statement?" she said, returning the flask to her pocket. "Back at Harvard, Billy slit his wrists. He'd always had a tough time fitting in. Kids would pick on him for having a speech impediment, and by the time he got it fixed with a therapist, he was behind the curve socially. Jane was just his friend at the time, coming to his room to ask if he'd want to go out with some of her friends that night. He was still pretty socially awkward back then, but she always made an effort to include him. She saw his door cracked open ever so slightly and opened it up to find him holding his hands out over a trashbin, watching himself bleed dry. She called 911, saved his life."

Chang glanced at the chandelier hanging above the foyer. "They'd been dating for a few years when I met him and got married shortly after that. Fun wedding."

"What happened to her?" Sydney asked.

"She died of an aggressive form of brain cancer almost five years ago. After that, he started spending more and more time here." She gestured around the lodge. "The reserve is one of the few things he has that he still seems to enjoy. That, and hunting of course. He's been here three years now, and I don't know if he'll ever leave. Richard sure as hell won't." She drew her flask again as she started walking back towards her room. "Have a good evening."

Then she vanished around the corner.

"I want to get in that room," Sydney said. She was staring into the pool, illuminated bright blue by LED lights under the water, her arms wrapped around her legs as she sat on a lawn chair near the edge. It turned out there was a nice breeze tonight, so they hadn't had to worry about bugs after all.

Andy was sitting beside her. "Why?"

"I feel like there's an answer in there."

"An answer to what?"

"I don't know."

"Sydney, you're acting paranoid."

"Jones is dead–"

"And that's terrible. He seemed like a nice enough guy, but it was an accident."

"The night before he went out, I heard him and Chang talking about something Sans wasn't showing us in the labs. There was some secret entrance to it he was going to check out, and you had to enter it from a cave."

"That sounds…," he began, then seemed to reevaluate his opinion halfway through the sentence, "admittedly suspicious."

"They were talking about some new project Sans is working on and how it's gone way over budget. The board is breathing down his neck. I think that's the real reason this two-week gig was set up: they needed an excuse to send executives out here in person. When you think about it, for our skill sets, we've been doing some pretty menial tasks. I mean, tagging animals?"

"It's part of what a zoologist does. Also, you're getting to handle cutting edge microchips that haven't hit the market yet. You get to see how they field test things."

"But for an *entire week*? And what have you been doing?"

"We've been reviewing the data sent in. The computer systems map it mostly and my supervisor tells me what to look for, pretty much."

"But the labs have some of SansCorp's best tech, and we're not being allowed to see it. None of what we're doing requires that much thought."

"It doesn't matter the reason we're here, Sydney. At the end of the day, we should be grateful that we got an all-expenses-paid trip to Africa for two weeks and that, major bonus, it happens to look fucking stellar on our resumes. We've got another week, so let's not screw this up like Courtney did."

She sighed. There was a moment of silence, save for the

water lapping gently at the side of the pool.

Then Andy got up. "I'm going to sleep. We've got a day off tomorrow and then we switch jobs up on Monday, so let's just take it slow. This is the halfway point, and in a week, it'll all be over. Just remember that. Good night."

He left. She lay back in her chair and stared up at the stars for a few minutes, mulling things over in her mind. Her fever started to come roaring back with a vengeance. It was time for the painkillers.

Groggily, Sydney got up and went inside. After she turned past the landing at the top of the stairs and began walking down the hall to her room, she suddenly stopped.

The door to what had been Courtney's room was ever so slightly ajar. That was odd. She'd been sure it had been closed completely earlier. Looking behind her, no one was around. Out of curiosity, she inched forward and reached for the handle. There was a slight *creak* of the hinges as she pushed the door open, taking a step into the room.

Then she froze.

There was a suitcase on the floor, open with some clothes strewn about. She was pretty sure Courtney had worn that one top on Tuesday. The bed was unmade. A computer tablet sat on the desk. Beyond, the window overlooked the forest on the hillside, barely visible in the dark.

In that moment, Sydney forgot about her fever and the soreness of her muscles entirely, and darted out of the room to knock on Andy's door.

COURSE OF ACTION

"Now do you believe me?" she asked, standing in the doorway.

Andy completed a full circle look around the room. "Oh, this is bad. This is very bad."

"What do we do now?"

"We go back to my room. Quickly."

They stepped back into the hall and Sydney closed the door over very carefully. "Wait, should I leave it the way I found it or completely closed?"

"The way you found it."

"But someone clearly forgot to close it all the way and might think we–"

"Just leave it."

She put the door back in exactly the position she found it. Then she and Andy went into his room and shut the door.

Andy started pacing again. "Oh shit, shit, shit…"

"We need to get into the trophy room."

"Are you crazy? How?"

"Once he goes out into the reserve again tonight, we sneak in."

"But Sydney, the doors are locked."

"There's gotta be a key."

"I bet it's in his pocket."

"Well, what else can we do?" she said.

Andy ran his hand through his hair. "I don't know."

"One person is dead, another is missing, and they lied to us about her leaving. We don't even know if Sans was telling the truth about how they found Jones!"

"Christ, you think they killed him?"

"I don't know," she said. "Maybe."

Andy put a hand to his forehead. "Fuck."

Suddenly, an idea popped into her head. "You know how there's a skylight on the roof?"

"Yeah?"

"How come we've never seen it from in here?"

His eyes lit up. "It's over Sans's room."

"Exactly."

"You're not thinking…"

"We could easily climb up to the roof from the balcony. Then we open the skylight and climb down."

"What is this, *Mission: Impossible*?"

"There's rope in the garage. I saw it yesterday. You could hold it while I climb down and unlock the door from the inside."

"This is a bad idea. What if we can't even open the window from the outside?" he said.

"Then we break it. There's no alarm system and most of the staff will either be out with him, in the lab, or two floors below."

"Then they'll know we've been in there."

"Andy, do you honestly think Sans is planning to let us leave this place alive?"

He was silent for a moment. "We need to tell Brandon."

"He's sick."

"He needs to know what's going on." Andy brushed past her and cautiously creaked the door open. After making sure the coast was clear, he went across the hall and knocked on Brandon's door as Sydney watched from the doorway. There was silence as Andy waited for an answer. Nothing came. He knocked again. "Brandon? You there?" Dead silence.

"It's just us now," she muttered.

"Everyone's dropping like bloody flies around here," Andy said, storming back into his room. She shut the door. "Okay," he continued, "we do your idea. But how will that help us get out of here?"

"What's the only way off the reserve?" she said.

"The plane, pretty much."

"And who do we know who can fly planes?"

"Chang," he said, suddenly recalling.

"And the only way to convince her is if we get some hard evidence of whatever the fuck is going on here," she said.

"You thought of all this?"

"Just now."

Andy paused for a moment. "You don't think Chang's in on it, do you?"

"I doubt it. Sans wouldn't even let her see his trophies."

"Alright," he said. "We do it. What's the next step?"

"Now," she said, "we wait."

TRESPASSING

Sitting on the edge of her bed, Sydney put a hand to her forehead. She was getting warm again. The two aspirin she'd taken forty-five minutes ago hadn't seemed to kick in yet. The soreness throughout her body was now a throbbing ache, a pain that seemed to pulse through her. She was, in no circumstances, feeling ready to climb atop the roof of a two-story building and infiltrate a locked room through a skylight like a cat burglar.

But as she stared out the northern-facing window in her room, waiting to watch two pairs of rear lights vanish into the black of night, she realized she had no other choice. She would either find the answers to her questions or soon enough they would find her, and that potentially meant ending up like Jones or Courtney. Or Brandon.

"Anything now?" Andy said, lying on the bed behind her.

"Not yet," she said, glancing at the clock. 10:57. At this rate, Sans was going to leave later than the night before. Off in the distance, she could see lightning flashes amidst storm clouds. That was rare, she thought. They were currently in the Serengeti's dry season, but storms still passed through occasionally. Regardless, the clouds were heading their way, and getting close.

"What if they don't go out tonight?" he asked.

"We'll cross that bridge if we come to it."

"At what point to do we start discussing a second option?"

"After midnight."

He nodded. She was starting to feel hungry again. In her dorm room, she always had enough snacks lying around–

There they were. Two Land Rovers, driving off into the plains of the savanna. "They left," she announced.

Immediately, they bolted upright and headed for the door. They'd talked through the plan multiple times for the past couple hours. First, they carefully made sure no one was out in the hallway. Then they quietly proceeded past the landing and inched down the stairs. Sydney looked right towards the garage and staff quarters while Andy checked the dining room. They made sure each was clear before proceeding.

They turned right towards the garage and slowed down as they approached the staff rooms corridor. Sydney peered around the corner. Empty. Then they went into the garage itself.

Once inside, Andy immediately turned on the lights and grabbed a flashlight off the table to his right. Sydney went to the left and looked at the spools of rope. "This is probably about thirty feet," she said, examining one.

"That's more than enough," he said. "We don't know when they're going to get back. Let's go."

She threw the spool over her shoulder and then opened the door ever so slightly. Clear again. They moved briskly back into the foyer and up the stairs. Then they made a hard left and crept through the eastern wing of the guest bedrooms, finally reaching the glass door to the second-floor balcony.

Sydney squinted and tried to make out any figures lounging on the chairs. No one. *Good*, she thought. *Smooth sailing so far*.

Opening the door, she led Andy outside to where the railing met the exterior wall of the lodge. Directly above, the balcony overhang connected with the rest of the faux-straw roof. Thunder roared nearby. The storm was getting close.

"We better move quickly," she said, putting one foot up on the railing. Then she grabbed hold of a wooden support beam and climbed up, turning to grab onto the roof itself. However, she couldn't get a good enough of a grip on it to pull herself up alone. "I'm going to need you to lift me up," she called down.

Andy leaned over the railing and looked towards the ground. "This is a bad idea."

"You got a better one?"

Reluctantly, he wrapped his arms around her legs and heaved upward. Her torso cleared the roof's edge and she grasped for leverage. Suddenly, she felt a drop of water land on her forearm. Then another. She glanced at the clouds now blowing in directly overhead. Rain was beginning to gently drip down from above. *Not good*, she thought as she placed her left foot on Andy's shoulder and pushed herself up further. She brought her right leg up to where the two parts of the roof met and wedged her foot in the vertex as hard as she could to help push the rest of her body up on top of the structure.

The slant of the overhang wasn't too steep, so she didn't have to worry about sliding off, but at the same time she didn't have a strong hold on anything. The ridge was just a few feet out of reach. Carefully, Sydney got onto her knees and began crawling up towards it. She stretched out her hand and grasped it; it would have to do.

"Okay," she called down. "I'm up."

"Alright, now what do I do?" Andy shouted. "I'm going to need some help."

While keeping her left hand firmly gripped on the ridge, Sydney slid down as far as she could and held out her right hand. "I'm ready."

Andy's right arm made it up the roof, the flashlight grasped in his fingers. His other hand was still holding the support beam. The wind and rain were both picking up now. She could hear the trees rustling nearby as he started to bring his leg up to the vertex between the main roof and the overhang.

Once in a reasonably secure position, he said, "Take the flashlight." She grabbed it from his outstretched hand and shoved in the side of her shorts. Then she reached down for him again as he detached his grip from the support beam and swung his left hand around to grab hold of hers.

She seized his hand just as a massive boom of thunder sounded overhead and his lower body slipped.

The next thing Sydney knew, most of Andy's body was dangling in the air and his entire weight pulled on her grip. She could feel her grasp on the ridge straining, the rain now mercilessly pelting at every inch of her body. Water flowed down the roof and fell past Andy to splatter on the patio below. If she lost hold, she knew both of them would be doing the same.

Her muscles had been hurting already, but with this it was too much. Sydney clenched her teeth and pulled him up with all her might. Andy managed to bring his leg up and let go of her to scramble for the ridge. He nearly slipped once more, but managed to reach the crest a moment later.

Andy turned to her and laughed. "What the fuck are we doing?" he shouted over the rain.

"Beats me."

"You got the rope still?"

She gestured her head towards her other shoulder, where the spool was resting.

"Now what?" he asked.

"We make our way over there along the ridge," she said, pointing through the torrential downpour towards the main roof itself. There was a flat area at the top where the skylight was positioned above Sans's quarters.

Andy started shimmying along the ridge and she followed. *Slow and steady*, she told herself. There was no rush. She glanced out towards the expanse of the reserve to see if she could spot returning headlights, but she could barely glimpse anything in the storm. There was a streak of lightning through the sky a few miles away and the loud rumble hit them just as Andy climbed up past the crest and onto the top of the main roof.

He turned around and extended his hand. "We have to be careful of the lightning," he said, taking her arm and pulling her up. "This is the tallest structure around here."

"No," she said, pointing up the hill to the plateau where the landing strip was. "That is." A radio communications tower was mostly obscured by the night and rain, but a red light blinked at the top every couple of seconds.

Crouching, they made their way over to the skylight, which was positioned along the north-south axis of the lodge. Sydney examined it: there were three windows on each side of the triangular prism-like structure, but only the middle appeared to be able to be opened. She pressed her face to the glass and looked down. The room was dark save for one lamp on a stand along the western wall below and to her right.

Seeing no reason to delay, she grabbed the handle at the base of the central window and pulled it up. It was locked. She saw there was a latch to her right and slid a thin metal bar out of place, then pulled up again. This time the glass pane opened upwards into the rain.

She handed the rope to Andy and he began to unfurl it and lower one end into the dimly lit chamber. Turning on the flashlight, she watched the rope descend to the floor roughly twelve feet below. "Stop, that's good enough," she said, handing the light to him.

Andy took it and braced his legs against the skylight. Then he leaned back, ready to hold the rope as tightly as he could. He wiped rainwater from his eyes, then gave her a thumbs up.

Slowly, Sydney slid her legs under the retracted window pane and, tugging on the rope to make sure it was taut, began to lower herself over the edge. *This really is a bad idea*, she thought as she began climbing down one hand over another. *Steady, steady...* Her fever was starting to return, the ache in her muscles seeping back through her body. Trying to ignore the pain, she glanced down. The bottom was just seven feet below. *I could jump that–*

Then she slipped.

The dark floor rushed up to meet her. Sydney managed to bend her knees on impact, but it was by no means a controlled landing. She tumbled over and came to rest on her back, the breath suddenly taken from her.

"Are you alright?" Andy called down through the skylight.

"Yeah, I'm fine," she said, struggling to get to her feet. She hadn't hurt herself too badly and nothing was broken, which was good.

"Can you unlock the door? I'm going to come back down."

"Be careful!" she called.

"Nah, I thought I'd break my neck. Just to see what it's like."

She rolled her eyes and extended her middle finger upwards.

"Love you too," he called. The window was slammed shut back into place and he disappeared from view.

Sydney exhaled and looked around. In the dim glow of the lamp, she could just make out that the walls had neat wood furnishings. There was a large window at the far end and she could make out some kind of bedframe and a desk back there too. She had no clue where the light-switch was though; Andy had taken the flashlight.

She wondered if he was still on the roof or if he had gotten back to the balcony safely yet. Lowering oneself down was easier than climbing up, but it was still, quite literally, a slippery slope.

Sydney put a hand to her head. She was burning up again and the painkillers didn't seem to be working anymore. In a daze, she stumbled backwards, knowing the door had to be behind her somewhere. She just needed to undo the lock, let Andy in, and then they could start to figure out what the hell was going–

Lightning flashed directly above the lodge. In a fleeting burst of brightness, the room revealed itself to her. But the only thing she could focus on us for that brief instant was the head mounted on the wall across from her.

She glimpsed a hideously terrifying face, viciously sharp teeth, and crimson pupils forever locked in a death glare into the void.

Then the darkness returned as thunder shook the building and reverberated through her bones.

MONSTERS

Sydney covered her mouth, stumbling back through the blackness. Her eyes remained fixated on the point where she had seen the dead creature until she suddenly hit a wall. No, that was a handle she felt against her back. It was the door.

Pain shot through her body. Her forehead felt as if it was about to burst into flame. And now her mouth suddenly hurt too, an ache slithering into each of her teeth. Her back pressed against the entrance, she slid down to the floor and took her head into her hands, trying to focus. The lamp seemed so far away and she was lost over here, in the dark, surrounded by the faces of things she couldn't see.

She remembered a time in third grade, when several girls had locked her in a dark closet and told her monsters were going to eat her. Of course, she was long over that, but seeing the sharp teeth and red eyes had awakened an old fear. *Keep it together, it's dead.* But something Chang had told her tugged at that back of her mind. This was a trophy room, which meant there was surely more than one of those things in here.

Huddled against the wood and drenched from the rain, Sydney tried not to think of the monsters or her headache or her muscles or her teeth and took several deep breaths. She started shivering and realized she needed to dry off or she'd probably get pneumonia. *Add that to my list of problems,* she thought.

Surely Andy was supposed to be here by now. Had he fallen? Was he okay? How long did she have to wait before going out to find him? She wondered if she should run back to her room quickly anyway, just to grab more painkillers. No, she could overdose. But she knew she wouldn't be much use helping Andy if she could barely think straight–

There was a knock, startling her out of her reverie. Then she realized it was someone rapping on the door, right behind her. "Sydney, it's me," she heard Andy whisper.

"Hold on," she muttered, getting to her feet. She blindly felt around in the dark for the handle. Then she groped beneath it for the lock, found it, and turned it sideways. There was a *click* and she stepped back as Andy quickly opened the door and swung through.

"Any trouble?" she asked as he shut and locked it behind him.

"No," he said, turning on the flashlight and illuminating the space between them. "Are you alright?"

"I'm fine, but I need to show you something."

He stared closer at her through the light. "Sydney, what's wrong with your eyes?"

"Nothing," she said, irritated. "Give me the flashlight." She grabbed it out of his hands before he could, then slowly moved the beam across the far wall.

"What is–?"

"Just wait," she said. He went quiet and the only sounds she could hear were the raindrops on the skylight and her slow, deep breaths. As the beam slowly worked its way up the wall towards where she knew it was, she could feel her heart beating faster in her chest. *You've already seen it*, she told herself. *You know it's there.*

The light moved over the hunting trophy. Everything above the base of the creature's neck was mounted to a wooden plaque. The head was massive, seemingly bigger than a lion's but sharing the same mane around its collar. Its face wasn't regal or majestic however; instead, it featured the brutishness of an ugly hyena with a dark, dog-like snout. Still, she realized, there was a distinct lion-ish feel to its appearance that she couldn't quite place. Its jaws were agape, displaying fangs like daggers. They were unlike any teeth she had seen in an animal before; the canines had to be at least four inches long. Even without the initial shock of seeing it for the first time, she still found it plenty disturbing.

Andy stepped closer. "I take back what I said earlier. This place is fucked."

"I think it's safe to assume this is what killed the elephant and the wildebeest."

"And Jones," he added. She remembered what Sans had said about finding his remains and looked at the teeth. It sent a shiver down her spine. "What the hell is that thing?" Andy asked.

"It must be some kind of transgenic hybrid," she said, thinking out loud.

"And he created it for what? *To hunt for sport?*"

"I think so." She shone the beam around the room. There were other creatures similar to that one, although not all of them had manes. She guessed they were male and female, which made sense if these things had lion genes.

"Why would they let us out in the day with these things

around?"

"I think they're nocturnal. It must be why Sans only hunts them at night."

"You think this was the secret project Jones was talking about?"

"Must be," she said, sweeping the light towards the back of the room. She started towards the desk, which was against the western wall. There were several neatly arranged stacks of paper and a large touchscreen monitor. A sleek LED desk lamp was positioned on one side; she turned it on and handed the flashlight to Andy.

Moving to the computer, she touched the power button on the side and watched it quickly boot up. She had been hoping there'd be no password since only Sans had access to the room, but that proved to be wishful thinking the second she got to the log-in page.

"Shit, any idea what his password might be?"

Andy was shining the flashlight around the room, still examining the mounted heads. Then he came upon something else and stopped. "Sydney, look."

She turned around. On each side of Sans's bed were dozens of framed photographs of Sans and a woman. She realized that must've been his wife, Jane. She walked closer to the wall, taking them all in. Each of the photographs was labeled. There the two of them were on the Serengeti, SCUBA diving in the Seychelles, at the summit of Kilimanjaro. They looked so happy together. Sydney peered closer to look at Jane. With jet black hair and emerald eyes, she was several inches shorter than Sans, but her posture and smile suggested more confidence. Sans looked very happy in each of the images, standing beside her or with his arm around her waist.

As she gazed at their wedding photo, a thought suddenly popped into her mind. She turned back to the computer. "That's it."

"What's it?" Andy said, following her.

"I read somewhere that people who have lost loved ones tend to use their names as passwords." She quickly typed "janesans" into the log-in bar and the words "Incorrect Password" came up. Frowning, Sydney tried "JaneSans", "Janesans," and "janeSans". The last one worked.

She was in. The desktop background was a magnificent Serengeti sunset. Clicking on the file explorer icon on the bottom taskbar, Sydney went into Documents and found a folder labeled "SansCorp". Opening it, she was presented with several more subfolders.

> Admin
> Facilities
> HR
> Operations
> Research

"Do you think it would be under Operations or Research?" she asked.

"Try Research," he said.

She clicked it open and found another set of files, this one much longer. She found herself scrolling down through a vast list of topics ranging from research papers to animal test subject BAM and SAM files.

"What's that?" Andy said over her shoulder, pointing to one. She tilted her head, making sure she was reading it correctly.

It said: "Interns".

She tapped it open. Inside were four different PDF documents, each with their names. She tapped open the one labeled "Marlowe, Sydney" and started scrolling through the pages.

"Hey, here's my work history, all of my medical records, and...a psychological profile? He even has stuff on my family here too!" she said.

"What the hell does he need this stuff for?" Andy said, leaning closer.

From across the room, there was the sound of a doorknob being jiggled. Then someone banged on the door.

"Hey!" called a voice. "Who the hell is in there?"

GETAWAY

Standing at the computer, Sydney froze. The knocking came again, this time louder.

"We know you're in there and there's no other way out," the voice said. They sounded distinctly South African.

"Now what?" she hissed to Andy.

He spun around wildly, shining the flashlight all around the room. "I don't see any other exit. Wait." He pointed to the window. "We could climb down."

"Are you crazy?" she said.

"You just broke into a madman's office by climbing through a skylight."

"Did you bring the rope?"

He showed it to her slung over his shoulder. "I don't think there's time though," he said, running to the window and starting to open it. The sounds of pouring rain filled the room. Andy motioned for her to go first. Sydney ran over to the sill, sliding her leg over and out into the deluge outside. She groaned, not excited about getting soaked again.

Still, as she lifted her other leg up and turned over onto her stomach to slowly lower herself into the rain, she knew she had no choice. She was dangling above the rear entrance to the lodge. She was about fifteen feet up.

Her upper torso was still on the window sill. She looked at Andy. "We should use the rope."

"No time," he said, pointing to the door. The banging was getting louder. "We gotta move."

Sydney's headache was only getting worse and for some reason her teeth were killing her too. She grunted and let herself down as far as she could, her fingers clenching the edge of the window.

Then she dropped.

This time, she expected the fall and sufficiently braced herself for the impact. The landing still jolted her, however, and it took her a moment to regain her bearings. Andy dropped down quickly after and grabbed her arm.

"Run!" he said as they took off towards the treeline.

She glanced back to see a silhouetted figure reach the second-story window and point after them. "They're heading for the forest!" she could hear them call.

She and Andy followed the path into the dark cluster of trees. It was pitch black here as Andy led her off the path. She heard Andy trip, but he appeared to get back up quickly. She stumbled forward blindly, keeping her arms out to make sure she didn't run into a tree. She brushed past several trunks and noticed the terrain getting steeper beneath her feet. They were heading up the hill.

They continued like that for a minute or so before she

stopped to catch her breath. It felt as if her heart was in her throat, and despite taking multiple deep breaths, she didn't feel her exhaustion lightening. The rain continued to pelt her skin.

"Where are you?" she said.

"Over here." He sounded about six or seven feet away.

She started towards him, putting one foot before the other, but suddenly lost her balance on the uneven ground and fell down the hill. She tumbled several feet and came to a halt. Everything hurt, but she couldn't tell if it was inside or out.

"Sydney?" he called out.

She felt around for the slope of the muddy ground, trying to tell which way was up. "I'm coming," she said. She kept low, using her hands to scope out the hill as she moved. Eventually, she pulled herself up next to a tree, figuring she had to be near him. "Are you there?"

"Right here," he said. He was just a few feet away. Perfect. "I'd have used the flashlight, but I didn't want to risk it."

"What's the plan now?"

"I think we have bigger problems. Look."

Peering out from the tree, she glanced towards the bottom of the hill. Disembodied beams of light swept through the darkness about fifty feet away. They were getting closer, but still appeared to be moving along the path. She counted the lights. There were three of them. She knew a few staff members would be out with Sans on the hunt and the others would probably be in the laboratory. So, hopefully, these three staff members would've been the only ones in the lodge.

She pressed herself against the wet bark, trying not to think about the ghastly trophies in Sans's rooms, as one of the lights danced momentarily in their direction. Once it had passed, she turned to Andy. "We need to get back to the lodge."

"Why?" she heard him hiss.

"I think they're all out here."

Two of the lights had vanished into the forest on the other side of the path, but one was now coming closer. She couldn't see the person wielding it at all.

"Okay," Andy whispered.

Sydney watched the levitating beam begin to search the area about twenty feet in front of her, now illuminating the ground and scanning for footprints. Now was their chance. Slowly, she started moving to the left. The light was still facing a different direction from her, the torrent of rain visible everywhere it turned.

There was a soft patter of footsteps nearby and she knew Andy was right behind her. Her eyes had adjusted enough that she could make out the shapes of trees, which helped guide her as she started moving quicker and lower to the ground. Grabbing Andy's hand, she pulled the two of them behind a trunk close together as the light shone upon where they'd been hiding earlier. The floating beam glided closer to investigate.

She looked to the left. The other two lights were distant specks swinging around in the dark. The third man was now ten feet off to their right. Any second now, he'd turn the beam in their direction and–

"Run," she hissed.

"What?" he whispered.

"Now!"

She sprinted forward down the hill, dodging past tree after tree, snapping twigs beneath her feet. Andy was right alongside her.

Swiftly, a light was shone on them from behind. "They're over here!" a voice screamed.

Up ahead, she could see the forest coming to an end and the lights of the lodge beyond. As she and Andy emerged from the treeline, they broke into full sprints towards the back doors of the house. She could hear voices and shouts somewhere behind her but didn't care to listen. The cold rain pelted her skin so hard it hurt, her heart pounding in her chest as the doors got closer and closer until–

Sydney grabbed the handle and threw it open wide. "Get in!" she shouted at Andy and he swept past her a split second before she yanked the door shut and fumbled with the lock until it slid into place. She looked up. Three running shadows were halfway behind them on the back field, their flashlights waving wildly as they drew nearer.

"Go around the front!" she heard one of them yell and saw the group split up, two going around one side and the third the other way.

Immediately, she ran out of the library and down the corridor to the foyer. Thanks to her wet sneakers, she slipped on the wooden floor but caught herself as she went down, barely even dropping speed. Sydney darted to the front double doors and put her arms out in front of her as she slammed against the wood. Immediately, she reached above the handle and locked it.

Andy watched as she slid to the floor, her back against the doors. "Are there any other entrances?"

"I don't know," she said, gasping for breath and pushing wet hair out of her face. Then she realized something and shot to her feet. "It doesn't matter, Sans will be back soon." She sprinted down the hall to the garage, threw the door open, and turned on the lights.

"What are you doing?" Andy asked, watching as she grabbed a key fob off the rack and tossed it to him.

"You drive," she said, clutching her forehead. After the burst of adrenaline, her symptoms were starting to catch up with her – and now she was feeling even worse. She managed to stumble around to the back of the nearest Land Rover and yanked its plug free.

"Where are we going?" he said, climbing into the driver's seat.

She hauled herself through the passenger door and pulled it shut after her. "Fucking anywhere, let's go."

He pressed the ignition button and the vehicle hummed to life, the front lights flaring on. Sydney feebly did up her seatbelt as Andy pressed the button above his head to retract the garage door while doing up his. Outside, she saw one of the staff members run into the headlights, arms out front to tell them to stop. His white polo shirt was dirtied with mud, his face snarling in anger.

Andy slammed his foot on the accelerator and the SUV shot forward, rain splashing across the windshield as the garage gave way into the night. The man dived out of the way at the last second. Then the vehicle swerved down the path and raced off into the grassland.

He put the wipers on as Sydney pressed her forehead against the window beside her, feeling the cool glass ease the heat from her skin. Groaning, she slowly opened her eyes and watched the lights of the lodge recede in the side mirror. She felt her shoulders begin to relax until she noticed two small pairs of headlights pulling away from the garage.

"They're after us," she muttered.

"I know," Andy said, glancing in the rear-view mirror. The Rover began to speed up, the suspension jolting more with each bump. Mud occasionally sprayed up along the sides of the car.

Lightning flashed in the storm clouds behind the other vehicles, which were steadily gaining on them. Sydney looked ahead and could faintly make out a small forest in the distance, just under a mile away. They were nearing the bridge and from there, the rest of the reserve would be wide open.

Just then, a sharp pain shot through the front of her jaw. It felt as if someone had jabbed pins deep into her gums below and above the canines. She clutched her mouth, then realized her right hand was shaking involuntarily.

"Are you okay?" Andy was looking at her with concern.

"Just drive," she grunted, checking the mirror. The pursuing Rovers weren't far behind in the rain, but now she could see the path through the small forest before them. They shot forward along the road, suddenly flanked by trees on both sides. The rain started hitting the windshield in more irregular patterns. The bridge appeared dead ahead, less than a hundred feet away now.

Andy glanced over at her. "What's happening to you?"

A set of headlights appeared over the bridge, heading straight for them. Sydney's eyes went wide and she pointed: "Look out!"

Andy saw just at the last second and swerved to the right as they reached the wooden structure. The ground gave way beneath the wheels as they cleared the riverbank and the vehicle briefly sailed through the air.

Then they hit the water.

RIVER

The entire vehicle was jolted by the impact and airbags went off all around the interior cabin. She felt the strain of her seatbelt holding her back and heard the rush of the river as it swirled around all sides of the Rover. Her body snapped back into her seat just as her eyes flashed open. The water level was rising past the windows and the car was leaning forward and slightly to the right as it sank.

The adrenaline rush was kicking in again, overriding the pain and soreness. She turned to Andy as he groggily rubbed his forehead and regained focus. "Shit, what do we do now?"

"We break a window and get out," he said, wiping blood from his nose.

"There could be crocodiles."

"We risk it."

The water went over the sunroof and the rainy surface was replaced with murky darkness all around as the tail end of the car slipped under.

"Sans's people are waiting on either shore," she said.

There was another jolt as the front wheels touched down on the riverbed, stirring up sediment that drifted past the windows.

He angrily smashed his fist against the horn, the resulting *beep* muffled by the water. "Shit."

"We could risk it with the crocodiles, maybe hold our breath and try to swim downstream for a bit. Then we get out and slip off into the forest."

"Then we're stranded in the Serengeti in the middle of the night? With those things Sans hunts running around?"

She glanced out the window. The moonlight wasn't even reaching them down here. "Then what are you saying?"

He sighed. "We let Sans take us."

"Are you kidding me?"

"They're going to be down here any minute now to fish us out. We go back to the lodge with them, then we figure out things from there."

"What if they kill us?"

"If they want us dead, all they have to do is leave us. Even if we escape the river, the two of us won't make it very far out here."

There was a sudden *thunk* on the window beside her. She was startled for a moment, then saw Ramsay's face peering through the window. He was holding his breath and motioning for her to get back. Then he brought up some kind of object she couldn't quite make out and slammed it against the glass. Cracks fractured outwards.

Quickly, she began undoing her seatbelt. Andy did the same.

With one final blow, the window shattered and dark water

and glass shards gushed in. She just had time to bring up her arms around her head and face protectively before the stream forced her back towards Andy, spilling over the center console and around the passenger seat into the second row and beyond.

The pair of them pressed their faces to the sunroof and took as many deep breaths as they could before the level rose above their heads. Sydney felt someone grabbing her arm and the next thing she knew she was being guided out of the submerged vehicle and upwards, back towards the surface as lightning flashed somewhere above.

A moment later, her head breached the water as she felt rain pelting at her skin once more. Ramsay hauled her ashore and quickly up the riverbank. Two of the staff were nearby with guns aimed at the water. She guessed they were checking for crocodiles.

Another man was bringing Andy out of the river. The pair of them were forcibly led over to where two Land Rovers were parked, their lighting rigs on full blast. Sydney had to shield her eyes as a silhouetted figure stepped forward, dressed in full hunting gear. A rifle was slung over his shoulder.

Sans marched forward and looked between her and Andy with disappointment. "You broke into my quarters, led my staff on a wild goose chase through a storm, then proceeded to steal and wreck my car." His British accent seemed more pronounced now. "After nearly a week of radio silence, I'm sure your parents will be just thrilled to hear of your exploits."

Sydney blinked to get some of the water out of her eyes, but other than that she didn't move. Her body felt terrible and on top of that her shoulders were so tense it was contributing to her headache. At least the rain felt cool on her forehead, but nobody had towels and she was standing there sopping wet, catching a chill.

"It's a shame," Sans continued. "You two were my

favorites."

He turned the men and jerked his head towards the cars behind him. "Let's get the hell out of here."

Andy was loaded into the backseat of one of the two Rovers, but Sydney found herself being walked by Ramsay in the direction Sans was headed – across the bridge where the two extra-equipped SUVs waited.

"Where are we going?" she asked feebly, an increasing sense of dread rising in her.

But Sans said nothing as they marched through the rain to the nearest vehicle. She saw a figure get out of the passenger side and walk around the back. Sans opened up the left rear door and gestured for her to climb in. She reluctantly did so, but as she sat down, the other figure suddenly appeared and jabbed a needle into the side of her neck.

Just as quickly as it was there, it was gone.

The door closed as she feebly reached for the spot of the injection, gently rubbing her stinging skin. Ramsay got into the driver's seat, Sans rode shotgun, and the other worker climbed in beside her. Everything started to get blurry as the electric motor whirred to life and the Land Rover started forward through the rain.

She began to black out when her right eye was suddenly forced open and a bright light was shone at her face. Then she felt a finger opening her other eyelid and the same procedure was repeated. After that she was finally allowed to lean against the window, feeling the crushing exhaustion overwhelm her. Voices were talking in the car, but they were muffled. Then everything was drowned out by the rain and she lost consciousness.

SPECIMEN

Sydney awoke slowly.

Everything seemed fuzzy around her as she sat up and put a hand to her head. She felt weird. Something was off about her. As her vision started to get back to normal, she took in her surroundings. The room itself was dark gray and dimly lit by LED bulbs that cast a blue glow. She was on some kind of operating table with an intravenous tube in her arm. There was a screen monitoring her vital signs off to her left, a table with scalpels and other medical tools off to her right. She looked down and saw she was wearing a light blue medical gown; she could feel her underwear on beneath it. No one was around and there was silence save for the hum of the air conditioning.

Then she heard it.

It came from far beyond the room, down the hallway,

emanating from some unknown corner of this place – wherever the hell she was. It snaked through the gaps in the door like a ghost and when it reached her ears, a shiver ran down her spine. Then it was gone. She had no idea what made it, but she knew what it sounded like.

The high-pitched, drawn-out cry of an animal in pain.

For a moment, Sydney froze but the room was silent again. The blue light above seemed to diffuse outward in a strange way and she tilted her head to look at it, lost in a trance. Suddenly, she shook her head to snap out of it. She was clearly drugged but at least she didn't feel that sore anymore. In fact, she felt numb and light.

Then she remembered her predicament. She had to get out of here. Clenching her teeth, she grabbed the base of the needle and abruptly yanked it out of her arm. The IV tube clattered to the floor and she saw it led to a bag of clear fluid dangling from the top of a metal stand with wheels.

Sydney brought her legs to the side of the bed and felt the cool floor beneath the soles of her feet as she stood up. She felt a little wobbly and had to put a hand on the bed to stabilize herself. Then, slowly, she moved one foot then another towards the door, carefully repeating the process until the handle was within reach. She opened it slowly.

Outside, the hallway had a similar metal-gray look to it and there were more bluish LED light strips running the length of the corridor. There were a series of pipes along the right wall. She looked both ways, each of which ended in a branching T-junction. She heard the noise again as it echoed towards her from the left. As if it were luring her in, she began to walk down the passageway in its direction.

As the sound faded, Sydney rubbed her arms and felt goosebumps on her skin. The end of the hall still seemed so far away. She swayed slightly from side to side and the path ahead of her tilted gently back and forth in her vision, the cerulean glow from above shining in her eyes. She felt hazy and part of her wondered if this was all a dream.

Then why haven't I woken up yet? Gently, she pinched herself. It hurt more than she'd expected it to, but the environment around her didn't change. She began to feel nervous, scared even, as the animal cry came around the bend even louder and clearly in more pain than before.

Gulping, she glanced behind her to make sure no one else was around. She was alone. Sydney continued alongside the wall to her right, occasionally putting her hand on the smooth metallic surface to maintain her balance. Eventually, she reached the junction. To her left, the corridor continued for only another ten feet before it came to what looked like a large circuit breaker box on the wall.

To the right, the hallway opened into some kind of dark, rocky cavern.

A cave.

The wail erupted again from somewhere beyond, beckoning her into the blackness. She followed, watching as the polished floor beneath her feet gave way to stone ground that had clearly been smoothed over by machinery. As she continued out into the cavern, everything got darker all around her but she could still see thanks to more electric blue light strips along the walls.

She was in an area about thirty-five feet wide and twenty feet tall with sharp stalactites dangling from the ceiling. Off to her right, the cave narrowed and a large metal gate blocked access to the rest of it, although there was a large security door with a glowing red keypad beside it. Across the cavern was another man-made corridor with the same metallic gray walls, ceiling, and floors.

From her left came a terrifying, hideous roar.

Sydney spun around. There were four sets of caged doors

along this side of the cavern. Through one of them, a pair of red eyes stared out at her and in the dim blue ambiance, she could make out sharp fangs biting at the bars. Another monster was in the cage beside it, gnashing its teeth and growling with feral intensity.

She turned and half-stumbling, half-running made her way towards the next hallway. She had gotten halfway across the space when a voice cried out: "Wait!"

Sydney turned around. In the third cage, clutching at the bars, was a person. As she stepped closer, she recognized their face.

Courtney.

"Holy shit, Sydney? Is that you?" she said, her voice quieter now.

Sydney ran up to the bars. "I saw your room earlier today. What the hell happened? They told us you left."

She looked on the brink of tears. "Those bastards kidnapped me. They injected me with something and then I woke up here. They're doing experiments with these weird fucking animals. Someone's always here and I don't even know what's day or night anymore. How long have I been here?"

"I think it's very early Sunday morning," Sydney said, rubbing her head. How long had she been out? There was no light down here so it could've been the middle of the day for all she knew. "So nearly four days."

"I think they're doing something to me," Courtney said, looking manic. "I can feel it in my bones. And I've had this fever non-stop."

The wail reached her ears again. Both she and Courtney looked in the direction of the other passageway.

"There they are. I don't know what they're doing or what the hell that thing is, I just want to get out of here."

"I'll be right back," Sydney said, moving away from the

cages. The hybrids were still snarling behind her but she figured the bars were well designed.

"Don't leave!" Courtney called after her. "We need to get out of here!"

But Sydney was barely even registering her anymore. Maybe it was just the drugs, but she felt inexplicably drawn to the creature's call. All other considerations seemed secondary at this point as she stepped onto the cool metal flooring and proceeded down the corridor.

It looked similar to the one she had been in before, but it didn't end in a T-junction. There was a laboratory with several large windows running the along the right side of the hall. Inside, it was dark save for the glow of several flat screen monitors. One of the computers closest to her appeared to be running some kind of gene sequencing program, but everything else was a blur in the background.

Along the left side of the hallway were two operating rooms. The first was dark but the lights were on in the second at the far end of the corridor, casting an ominous glow onto the floor. Again she heard the howl, but this time she could make out voices too, barely louder than whispers from here. She inched closer, a knot forming tighter in her stomach the nearer she drew. The voices became clearer.

"...get me more anesthetic."

"Preparing next charge."

Slowly, she peered around the corner and through the viewing window. About half a dozen people dressed in light blue medical scrubs were clustered around something on an operating table. There were several bright surgical lights positioned around them as they worked, but the rest of the room was dark save for the glow cast by several monitors. Three were along the back wall, showing x-rays and a mapping of what looked like a brain. Another two were observed by a sitting technician. At this angle, she couldn't see what was on them but the glow of the screens illuminated the man's face and his medical mask.

"Reed, I need you over here," a woman said. Sydney recognized her voice. It was Graves. Then a man moved and walked around the table towards her, suddenly giving Sydney a much better view.

Normally, her instinct would have been to turn away but instead she looked on in horrified fascination. The creature was over six feet long from its head to its feet. It had tan fur, a lion-like face, and sharp claws. That wasn't the odd part.

What disturbed her the most was that it looked almost human.

The thing lay on its back, fastened to the table by several sturdy-looking black leather straps, one of which was pulled tightly over its forehead. Beyond that, she saw that the skullcap had been removed and the brain was exposed. Graves was probing it with some sort of instrument she couldn't make out, but it appeared to be hooked up to whatever the technician was monitoring.

There were also electrodes with wires taped to various points all over the creature's body from its temples, pectorals, biceps, abdomen, and calves that she could see. She realized those were electrodes. The creature's eyes were fixated on the ceiling with jagged breaths coming from its mouth.

"Abdominal stimulant in three, two, one...," Graves announced.

The technician pressed something. There was a *zap* and the abomination spasmed, restrained by the straps. Its yellow eyes seemed to bulge out of its head and the same awful cry escaped its mouth.

"Muscle readings are good," the technician announced.

Suddenly, Graves looked towards her. In all her shock, Sydney hadn't realized that she'd stumbled out of her cover and was standing in full view of the window.

"Shit, get her!" the woman barked, pointing with a bloody gloved hand.

Sydney turned and ran back the way she came. Behind her, she heard the operating room door burst open and the sound of footsteps after her. She experienced a major head rush as she re-entered the cavern and nearly fell over. Clutching her brow, she managed to make it back to the original hallway and swerved left.

She didn't even know where she was going. She just knew she needed to get the fuck out of–

A gloved hand roughly grabbed her shoulder and pulled her back. Suddenly, two other technicians were restraining her as well. She could only vaguely make out who was talking behind their medical masks and the blue light beamed down from above as they lowered her towards the floor.

"Hold her steady," an American accent said, preparing a syringe.

"Please don't," she murmured.

"I told you she didn't have enough anesthetic, you idiot," a female voice, this one Kenyan, said.

"We didn't have enough time to check," the American said. "Graves said to hurry." Suddenly she felt the syringe enter the side of her neck. "Easy, easy," the man said.

"What are you doing?" came a familiar voice. Ramsay's. The three technicians' heads turned. From down the corridor, she heard loud footsteps striding towards them. "Get that out of her."

"We're re-sedating her," the American explained, carefully withdrawing the needle. "She got free while we were helping Graves with the–"

"It doesn't matter," Ramsay said. Dazed, she looked up to see him standing with military posture before them. Noticing she was conscious, he strode forward and bent down to look into her eyes.

"Dr. Sans wants to see you."

ITERATIONS

She seemed to faze in and out of consciousness through what happened next. The three technicians helped her into an elevator, then she was being led through a clean-white corridor that seemed somehow familiar to her. It was only once they were outside and in the rain that she realized they'd been under the veterinary labs the whole time, she'd just been too out of it to put it together. The cave should have been the giveaway.

Ramsay led them along the path with a flashlight as it wound through the forest. She could see the lights of the lodge through the trees up ahead. There was a rumble of thunder off in the distance, but overall the storm seemed to be lightening up. Finally, they walked out onto the patio and up to the front double doors of the building.

Inside, she was taken to the dining room where a lone

figure sat at the far end of the wooden table. It was Sans. He smiled when he saw her and gestured for her to take a seat. At the other end of the table, a plate with a heap of meat had been set with a glass of water.

"Please, take a seat," Sans said, gesturing to the chair. "You must be famished."

As she sat down, she suddenly noticed she was starving and began ravenously eating the ribs of some animal. She stopped, realizing she was using her bare hands.

Sans laughed. "Oh, it's alright. Go ahead." He watched her carefully as she continued. "You're probably worried about Andy, but don't worry, he's quite alright."

She ate in silence for a few minutes and Sans watched her with measured fascination. She had cleaned half the plate when she paused to down the entire glass of water. She wiped her mouth and said, "Do you mind if I ask a question?"

"Not at all."

"What the fuck is going on here?"

Sans smiled. "It's complicated, but I'll explain. One of the downsides of being here, so far from civilization, is that I have so few with whom I can share my excitement with."

"I saw the trophies."

"I had assumed," he said. "But do you know what they are?"

"If I had to guess, I'd say you spliced lion and hyena genes and grew an embryo in an artificial womb."

"Not quite. It's best if I start from the beginning. The *very* beginning." He folded his hands on the table and glanced out at the window. Raindrops rolled down the glass. "As you know, my parents brought me here all the time as a child and taught me how to hunt. At school, I was never particularly good at making friends. My EQ was never as high as my IQ, and it didn't help that my speech patterns were…less than perfect. Hunting was the only thing outside of academics that I truly excelled at, and above that, enjoyed. High school, university, and years in the pharma and biotech industries came and went, but hunting was the one constant. Even now, since my wife's passing, it's all I can find joy in. There was only one problem."

Sydney stopped eating as he took a deep breath and drummed his fingers on the table. "It began to grow boring." Sans scoffed to himself. "I didn't think it could happen and I denied it for years. But it finally became clear to me as I dispatched a charging rhino with ease and felt not even a twinge of fear. Killing it felt rote, almost mechanical, like something I was programmed to do. Hunting isn't about killing, it's about *thrill*. Take that away and you're just watching things die at your own hand. There was no purpose in it anymore, no feeling that I was a lesser creature earning my survival against nature's finest. I didn't want to feel like a god, I wanted to feel like an animal.

"Initially, I was terrified. This wasn't long after Jane died, you must understand, and I had gone around the world to try and find the one thing I thought I had left. And at that moment, staring down at the dead rhino, I realized I'd lost that. The only thing left to do was look to science. The cloning project here was already underway as a proof of concept for the company, but I wondered if hybrid species would provide a new challenge. Sadly, they didn't. I tried exactly what you described. I originally went for wild-raised versions of hybrids you see at the zoos – the ligers, the leopons. These were certainly a step up, but after a time, they too began to lose my interest.

"For a time, I thought there was no animal nature could throw at me – not even any of the possible *Panthera* genus hybrids – that I couldn't defeat with minimal effort. I realized that since I had beaten the game, the only way to continue to play was by new rules – my rules."

He seemed almost happy, clearly delighting in telling her

all of this. "It was around the same time that my company really began expanding on the gene therapy front. That was a subject that had always interested me, the notion that you could change the genetic makeup of a living organism. For most scientists, it's a means to correct defects and cure diseases, giving hope to those who would otherwise spend their lives without any. In fact, had the technology been sufficiently developed at the time, it probably would have saved Jane's life. That was, of course, why I had SansCorp pursue it in the first place. Alas, all this effort wouldn't bring her back and my mind wandered to other applications for it, ones that would solve my personal dilemma. I saw it as a means to control evolution."

She paused from eating. The calmness with which he proceeded was becoming unsettling. "When you think about it, humans have already been doing something similar for thousands of years with selective breeding and domestication. I wanted to do the opposite, to make animals more dangerous and unpredictable than nature had ever intended. To make the biggest game even bigger."

"So you created the perfect prey," she said. *That's obviously where he's going with this.*

Sans almost chuckled to himself. "Sadly, no. I took some of the cloned lions I had here and began performing gene therapy on them to insert DNA from a mix of other predators, primarily the hyena and the leopard. Over time, I began incorporating specific hormones and hybrid DNA from ligers too, to increase the size."

"What did you use for the vector? A retrovirus?" she asked.

Sans looked impressed. "Close. A lentivirus, actually."

Sydney nodded. Viruses already had the ability to alter an organism's DNA, so when a virus was created to infect the host's cells with specific new genes, it could be used to correct errors in the genetic code. Retroviral vectors were already some of the most common and reliable forms of gene therapy, but lentiviruses (which were members of the *Retroviridae* family) could insert genes into non-dividing cells, which made them more effective. And, as with standard retroviruses, the genes they inserted could be passed onto the next generation.

"The trophies you saw in my office are from the latest iteration. They are…difficult to hunt, but far from perfect. The hormone imbalance from the new DNA has given them strange behaviors. They will often kill large groups of animals and not eat all of them simply as a display of dominance and to establish territory. I believe you came across an example of that earlier this week. They are excellent at seeing in the dark but cannot adjust their eyes well to daylight, so they are strictly nocturnal. There are twelve of them, and most live in the cave system that connects to the labs. We have a few in cages right now to run periodic tests."

"They killed Jones?"

"Dear Richard decided to take an evening stroll through the cave. He must've thought the entrance was still inside the electromagnetic boundary. He thought wrong."

"Have any ever gotten past the boundary?"

"No, they all have tracking implants that are monitored in the lab. In fact everything, the entire electromagnetic system including the exterior border, is run from there. Mercifully, we've never had a failure of any of the emitters. What I have created here is meant to stay here. If any of them ever got off the reserve, it would be catastrophic."

A silence hung between them for a moment. There was something else she wanted to ask, something that waned her appetite even as she continued eating.

"What was that thing on the operating table?"

"What thing?"

"I woke up and explored the cave. I saw what Nurse

Graves was doing to that thing."

Sans smirked. "I suppose I should tell you now that Nurse Graves is actually *Doctor* Graves. She has a PhD in Genetics from Columbia. As for that 'thing' you so eloquently referred to, that is the next iteration of my project. It took quite a lot of convincing to get the board to fund a new private gene therapy venture, but I promised them it had applications far beyond what I was doing here. And I suppose one day, it will."

"But what is it?"

"The evolution of big-game hunting. But you would know it best by what it *was*." A sly smile formed on his face. "I believe you knew him as Brandon."

Her heart skipped a beat. Suddenly, she didn't feel hungry anymore.

Sans found her shift in mood amusing. "You see Sydney, the hybrids kept me busy. They served their purpose, but I realized it was time to get even bolder. I needed a prey that possessed the intellect of the most intelligent species on Earth – which, as hard as it is to believe at times, is in fact us – with the primal instinct, claws, and teeth of the greatest predators walking the planet today. If I could insert the genes of different animals into a lion, why couldn't I do it to a human being?"

"To *hunt them for sport?*"

"You don't understand, Sydney. This is where the vanguard of science and hunting become one. This is an exciting frontier that we here, on this reserve" – he pointed his finger down to the ground – "are being the first to witness."

"But it's murder!"

"Murder? That's what they said about euthanasia. That's what they said about abortion. The truth is, murder is a subjective construct. You only believe that this is murder because that's what society has spoon-fed you."

"Euthanasia is a mercy kill, and abortion is when the thing

doesn't even know what it is yet. You're talking about taking a healthy person with a life, transforming them against their will, and then killing them just so you can mount their head on a wall!"

"That's a drastic misreading of my intentions, Sydney. Brandon is an experiment, and you can't have progress without experimentation." He appeared happy, as if they were discussing movies or sports. "All those rich dentists who come to this continent to find the thrill of their lives have no idea how pedestrian they are. My purpose is not to wipe out the last of the endangered species, but to create a new prey that will give me the perfect challenge I have longed for all my life."

Then he paused, his mood growing darker. "But sadly, Brandon is not the end of my search. You see, the lentivirus I gave him – which had mostly lion DNA – suffered some of the same hormonal issues as the standard hybrids, which explains his abrupt change in behavior earlier this week. He's feral and unpredictable, certainly a formidable foe, but not the challenge I'm looking for. I want something that mixes thought with instinct and I'm afraid Brandon has been reduced to mere impulses. The virus worked all too well. He has become, quite literally, an animal." His eyes watched his fingers drum gently on the wood.

Then he looked up. "The second specimen, however, has shown *much* more promise."

The icy grip of fear enveloped her. "Who's the second specimen?" she said softly, almost as if it were a statement rather than a question. She already knew.

Sans smiled as Ramsay said behind her, "Are the drugs really working that well? I would've thought she'd notice by now."

Suddenly, the little things she'd overlooked before became much more apparent. Her teeth were hurting again and her skin felt strange. She remembered how she'd scratched herself earlier giving a pinch and looked at her nails. They were turning black and starting to curl down like claws.

Jesus Christ, she thought. *This has to be a dream.*

The mirror was about five feet away on the wall to her left. Abruptly, she flew out of the chair and ran over to it, bracing herself for what she was about to see.

The whites of her eyes were diffusing into a golden color. In her open mouth, gaping in shock, she could see her canines elongating. There was a light layer of fuzz around her face and on her arms that she knew was fur growing in.

"Feeling in touch with your wild side, Sydney?" she heard Sans say. Her head whipped around to see him watching her panic with a smug smile. "Your psych profile said you're quite insecure, so I hope you take comfort in knowing you are now a marvel of genetic engineering."

She was ready to leap onto the table and gouge his eyes out when Ramsay roughly grabbed her from behind and she felt a needle being inserted into her neck. She spun around as he pulled away, starting to feel dizzy. Ramsay and the technicians watched her collapse to the floor with a detached look, as if she were some kind of animal.

Then they moved in and everything blacked out.

PART III

WILD

TRANSFORMATIONS

The next thing she remembered was waking up in a cell with rocky walls and a metal gate across the front. She was still in her medical gown. Beyond it, she could see that she was back in the cavern. She faded in and out of consciousness for a time, feeling pain all over.

Finally, she opened her eyes to find a figure standing on the other side of the bars. It was Sans, silhouetted by the blue glow of the LED lamps. She could just make out a wicked smile on his face.

"Pleasant dreams, Sydney?"

All she could manage was a groan as she rubbed her eyes, careful not to scratch herself. The exhaustion was almost unbearable. Every inch of her felt sore. She didn't think she could even get up off the floor.

"You're progressing marvelously. In a day or two, the transformation should be complete."

"What? To look like Brandon?" she asked, her voice feeling hoarse.

He laughed. "No, you were given a different virus, one with leopard DNA. It appears to lack the hormonal issues of the lion strain, but the phenotypical changes have taken longer to become apparent."

"But, how was I infected?"

"Your primaquine tablets never actually contained primaquine. You've been ingesting the virus every morning this week. If you had stopped a few days ago, your body might've been able to overcome it. But I'm afraid your DNA's been altered too much to go back now. Still, it's time for your daily dose."

Graves appeared beside him, punching something in on the keypad. The gate slid open and the two of them walked in. There was another technician standing guard behind them. As Graves stood over her, she could see her opening the pill bottle and taking out a tablet.

Sydney huddled back against the wall. "I don't understand," she said feebly. "Andy and Courtney were on antimalarials too. Why weren't they infected?"

"We never took them off doxycycline," Sans said. "We were going to switch them to the faux-primaquine this week when they took over field work while you and Brandon would conveniently disappear during your lab time. That way we could test out a version of the virus on a male and a female. And then the next week we would switch which gender got each strain. Andy was set to get the leopard virus, but we're waiting to make sure you turn out okay first."

"How the hell do you think you're going to get away with this?"

Sans laughed. "Sydney please, your parents were

informed last Thursday that all of you died in a horrific vehicle accident when a Land Rover was lost in the river. No one thinks you're still here. You inadvertently helped me by actually destroying one last night, so I'll legitimately have to buy a new one."

"But…Chang and Jones…"

"Were also reported dead," Graves said. "Before we even knew Jones had taken care of himself."

"I'm afraid none of you were ever leaving this place alive," Sans said.

"Open wide." Graves was lowering the pill down towards her. All she could think to do was shake her head. "There are two ways we can do this," the woman continued. Sydney said nothing. "Alright, we're doing it that way."

She motioned to the other technician to come in and Sans stepped back while the pair of them restrained her. They barely needed to; Sydney didn't have the energy to fight back.

With gloved hands, Graves pried her jaws open. "The teeth are really coming in," she said. Sydney tried to turn her head away, but the technician kept her facing up as the doctor placed the tablet on her tongue with her index finger and thumb.

Sydney bit down.

Graves swore and pulled her hand back. Both the latex and skin had been broken and blood trickled down the clear glove as Sydney spat the pill out. Graves smacked her across the face, retrieved the tablet, and tried to pry her mouth open once more.

Sydney kept her teeth firmly clenched as the technician peeled back her lips. Graves shoved the tablet down the side of her mouth and the technician gave her an opened bottle of water, which she brought to Sydney's front teeth and held upside down.

She struggled but they held her there. Liquid spilled down her cheeks and splattered on the floor, but still she refused. Graves's eyes stared into hers with a vicious intensity. Finally, the water bottle ran out. Sydney didn't move.

Graves leaned in closer. "If you don't swallow, I'm going to shove that pill down your throat with my bare hand."

Sydney spat the water back in her face. The pill tumbled to the ground again.

Angrily, Graves wiped her face off as she stood up and kicked Sydney in the stomach. She doubled over in pain, but the doctor's foot lashed out again. The technician backed up, but Sans merely looked on, amused.

Sydney groaned as Graves knelt beside her again and shoved the tablet into her mouth. She stood up again and kicked Sydney once more, this time slightly gentler. "Swallow it," the doctor hissed.

She siphoned as much saliva as she could and gulped, the pill scraping her throat on the way down. Graves got back down and pulled her lower jaw down to check for any sign of it. She turned to Sans. "Clear."

"Well, that took long enough," he said, walking closer to stare down at Sydney. "Get some rest. Dr. Graves will be back for you later. I'm afraid I have a business call." The three of them left the cage and Graves threw one glance back at her, malice burning in her eyes.

Then the gate closed over and Sydney was all alone.

She drifted off to sleep again and groggily awoke to the sound of the gate opening once more. Ramsay and Graves helped her to her feet, then led her out into the cavern. She heard the hybrids growling and biting at the bars as she was taken down the corridor to the left, where the operating rooms were.

Panic gripped her as she struggled in their grasp.

"Now, now," Graves said. "There's no need to worry. We're not going to cut your head open." She wasn't sure if that was meant to be reassuring.

They brought her into the first room on the left, where three technicians were already waiting around the operating table. A fourth was viewing the monitors. She put her feet up on the edge of the table to push back and was horrified to see that they were covered in fur and her toes had become sharp like a leopard's hind claws. She was too shocked to fight back as they gently turned her around, helped her out of her gown, and lay her on her back.

There was a mirror above her and she could see that the peachy fuzz of the night before had become a short coat of beige fur with black spot formations over her entire body. Her breathing quickened as she stared at the reflection of her eyes. Around the pupils, the color was completely a dim, golden yellow. Her other front teeth looked sharper now too, not just the canines.

They started strapping her down but she was too fixated on the mirror to do anything. She only snapped out of it when they fitted the IV tube into her arm and began placing electrodes on her arms, stomach, and legs. Only her underwear provided her with any sense of decency.

Graves fitted her medical mask on and came around beside her. "This is a test of muscle stimulation. Normally, it doesn't have to hurt so much, but after this" – she held up her bandaged finger – "I don't think Dr. Sans will object if I use a little extra voltage."

Ramsay placed the final two electrodes on each of her temples.

"Shall we begin?" Graves asked. Without waiting for an answer, she turned to the technician behind the monitors. "First test: abdominal."

There was an electric *buzz* and suddenly horrific pain shot through her midsection. Her entire core tensed up and she lurched against the straps, her mouth opening in a scream.

It was over just as quickly as it began. Her muscles

relaxed and she began hyperventilating.

"Excellent muscle response. Abdominal strength has increased twenty-three percent since the pre-trip physical," the man behind the monitor reported.

"Hear that?" Graves said, leaning closer. She was clearly amused by the terror in Sydney's eyes. "Cheer up, you're in great shape. Let's test the biceps next."

They continued shocking her all over her body for what felt like an eternity. Finally, when it was over, they let her sit up and put on a fresh gown. Ramsay and another technician held her arms as Graves led them back to her cage. Between everything that had happened in the last twenty-four hours and the fact that her family didn't even know she was alive, she was struggling to hold back tears.

It didn't work. Graves saw them welling up in her eyes after she punched in the gate code. "That's a good sign. Other than elephants, we're the only animals that cry when we're sad. So even though you're technically a subspecies now, I guess that means you're still mostly human."

She gave Sydney a big, smug grin and gestured for her to enter the cage.

Later, she tossed and turned on the hard floor while trying to get to sleep. But hunger gnawed inside of her, and it was all she could think about until she heard footsteps outside and crawled to the bars to see Ramsay walking by.

"When do I get fed?" she shouted.

He turned and walked over. "That is for Dr. Sans to decide. A well-fed predator doesn't make for good hunting."

"Fuck you!" she spat at him, rattling the bars as best she could.

Ramsay watched her with pity. "Those are titanium, so

good luck with that." Then he walked off.

Sydney leaned back against the wall and slid down, putting a hand on her stomach as it gurgled loudly. Her mood grew progressively more sour with each passing minute as she moved from trying to sleep in various parts of the space to pounding on the rocky wall angrily.

Eventually, she resolved to simply lie on her back, staring at the ceiling and listening to the noises of the cavern. Her hearing was much more astute now and she could faintly make out the consistent drip of water somewhere deep within the cave system. It lulled her into a trance and she was just finally beginning to drift off to sleep when several voices appeared, down the hallway to the right.

A few moments later, Sans appeared at the bars. "Hello, Sydney. I've brought you company."

He stepped aside to show Graves gripping the arm of a drugged-up Courtney as Ramsay worked the keypad. The gate slid open and the girl was pushed inside, collapsing to her hands and knees. The grating closed over again.

Sydney rushed over and gently shook her arm. "Are you okay?"

There was a thin layer of peachy fuzz on her face. Sydney could feel it on her forearm too. Courtney looked up at her weakly with fear in her yellowish eyes. "Sydney, I want to go home."

She turned to Sans. "What's wrong with her?"

"Her little stunt on Thursday forced a change of plans, so since we locked her up down here we figured we might as well begin her on the lion virus, which she was scheduled for this week anyway. Of course, we didn't know about the hormone imbalance and I already have Brandon to poke, prod, and dissect, so she's basically useless to me now."

Sydney's eyebrows narrowed. "Then what do you want me to do with her?"

The right side of Sans's lip curled upward in a sinister smile.

"I want you to eat her."

ETHICS

"What?!" Sydney said. "I can't do that!"

"Why not?" Sans asked.

"She's a person!"

"And you're an animal, Sydney. A carnivorous one, I might add. And when carnivorous animals are hungry and the opportunity to consume meat presents itself, they consume the meat."

Courtney scurried away from her, backing against the grate. "Get away from me!" she screamed.

"Jesus, look at her. She's pathetic," Graves said, eyeing the terrified girl with pity.

Sydney looked at her claws and retreated further into the cell, feeling the cool rock of the rear wall press against her back. "No," she said. "I won't."

"See," Sans said. "You changed your vocabulary. A moment ago, you said you *couldn't* eat her, but when I pointed out it is perfectly within your capability to do so, you said you *wouldn't*. You are acknowledging that you are making a conscious decision to go against your instincts. Therefore, you know that the choice lies with you."

Her stomach growled loud enough for Courtney to hear it, a look of even greater panic coming across her. Sydney glanced between her and the others beyond the gate.

"Look at it this way," Sans said. "You're a biology major. When you are experimenting, what do you do with the waste? You dispose of it. She's not a person anymore, Sydney. The outside world thinks she's dead. Therefore, she still exists only as a test subject, a test subject that has served its purpose. You won't be committing murder; she's no more than biological waste."

I could do it, she realized. It would just take one quick pounce to be over there, one second more to tear out her throat. She wouldn't feel anything after that. Courtney's nightmare would be gone with Sydney's hunger.

Then she snapped out of it, not horrified so much with what Sans was proposing but with the fact that she had even considered it.

"No," she repeated, flattening herself against the back wall. "No, no, no."

Sans sighed. "This is your only chance for food today, Sydney." She said nothing, glaring at him with her leopard's eyes. He shook his head. "So be it."

The gate opened and, grabbing her by the shoulder, Ramsay dragged Courtney out. The door closed over again before Sydney could even think of an escape. She watched as the girl was hauled to her feet and led across the cavern. It struck her as odd for a moment. He wasn't taking her back to the other corridor.

Then she realized.

Sydney ran to the bars, watching Ramsay bring Courtney to the cave access gate on the far side. "Wait, you can't!" she cried.

Sans turned to her. "You had your chance, Sydney. But in nature, nothing is left to waste."

Courtney was trying to get free, but Ramsay effortlessly held her back with one arm while punching in the code. His eyes scanned through the bars to make sure none of the hybrids were near, then he swung open the door and, keeping it that way with his foot, turned to grab Courtney with both arms.

She screamed as he roughly threw her through the opening and swiftly shut it behind her. Her face appeared at the gate a moment later, her hands wrapping around the bars.

"Please!" she screamed. "Please, I'll do anything!"

"It's not your fault," Sans said soothingly. "It really isn't."

There was the sound of something moving through the cave behind her and Courtney was suddenly pulled back into the dark, vanishing from view altogether. Sydney covered her ears and tried to drown out the screams as they echoed all around the cavern.

Abruptly, they ceased and were replaced with the tearing of flesh and the sickening crunch of bone.

ANSWERS

Ellie Chang lowered her book and checked her watch. It was nearly six, which meant dinner would be served soon. She hadn't seen Sans all day and was waiting for him to make an appearance. In fact, she hadn't seen much of anyone around the lodge save for a handful of the staff.

It annoyed her that Sans wasn't letting her talk to the board. He said it would be best for her to give them a complete summary of their discussions once she returned. He also said he had informed the board about Jones's death.

She exhaled deeply. Poor Richard. She'd told him not to go out there and yet he hadn't listened. She didn't know what he'd expected to find in the lower labs. Sans had always been a very private person and he was always secretive about his work.

Granted, the company was losing market share and its

CEO was but a specter in the upper ranks of management, lurking off in a far corner of the world to perfect "the next level of gene therapy". Over the years, he'd earned the board's trust, but this latest project was hemorrhaging money and he stubbornly refused to show the results. They would be revealed "all in good time".

But NASDAQ prices didn't believe in such philosophies. Quarterly reports had to entice investors just as much as promises for the long term. So they'd sent Chang because she was the CFO and she knew Sans well, and they sent Jones because he was a trusted Senior Vice President and had been openly skeptical of the CEO as of late. It was like fishing up north: the board must've figured they had someone who could break the ice with Sans and another who could haul him out of the water.

Chang herself had tried to explain to them time and time again that Billy Sans was a complicated, albeit very intelligent person. But during the excruciatingly long trip over, she'd begun to reflect on how many excuses she was making for an old friend. And friendship and business weren't supposed to mix.

For the first few days of the past week, she and Jones had talked with Sans about the direction of the company. He'd showed them around part of the labs and pitched them his vision beyond the current project: gene therapy completely free of the risk of cancer, advanced genome editing for disorder-free children, introducing cloned animals to the wild to bring endangered species back from the brink of extinction. Their competitors were working on many of these things, but Sans assured them the tech that had been developed here was half a decade ahead of theirs.

"Great," Jones had said. "When can we see it?"

Sans had simply smiled and replied, "Patience is a virtue."

Sitting here in the library, a book now folded on her lap, she wondered what the purpose of this trip really was. It had been Sans's idea to bring the interns here and the board had seen it as a golden opportunity to get some ground truth by having some executives tag along. But then Sans had insisted that Chang and Jones stay for the full two weeks – and have no contact with the outside world. Not that that seemed possible anyway. There was no WiFi and her phone had no signal here. She guessed Sans had his computers hooked up to some satellite connection, but he hadn't breathed a word of it to her.

"What is this guy's deal?" Marder, the COO, had asked her.

She had simply shrugged. "Billy's an odd duck. He likes to do things his way. To get around him, you've gotta pretend to play by his rules and beat him at his own game."

And that entailed her doing pretty much nothing for the past few days. There were only so many Serengeti sunsets she could gaze off into before she started to wonder what was going on. It was odd that Sans had such an elaborate underground extension of the veterinary labs and it was odd that the interns seemed to be doing such menial tasks. It hadn't been cheap to get them out here, but as always, she kept telling herself that this was Billy and that it would all become clear soon.

She glanced at the cover of the book. It was a slightly weathered edition of *The Man-Eaters of Tsavo*, which she found to be a surprisingly engaging read despite the Victorian prose. Patterson's descriptions of the horrific, real-life animal attacks were utterly chilling. It made her think about Jones's grisly end. *What a fucking idiot*, she thought, standing up and putting the book back on the shelf.

Yawning, she walked out to the main foyer and looked around. The evening sun was glistening through the windows and reflecting off the chandelier. She looked to her left and saw the chef, Fatou, setting the table with help from some servants.

"Excuse me?" she said, walking over. "Have you seen Billy around?"

"*Dr. Sans* will be here soon," Fatou corrected. "You may

take a seat and wait."

Please, I've known him for almost twenty-five years. She rolled her eyes as she walked to her usual chair. Once she was situated, she looked around at the empty table. *Where the hell is everyone?* Jones was gone, the Courtney girl had bugged out early, and she hadn't seen any of the other interns around since last night. Come to think of it, she hadn't seen Brandon for a few days.

She impatiently began twiddling her thumbs when she heard someone approaching and looked up to see Sans striding into the room. He seemed to be in a cheery mood.

"How's your day been, Ellie?"

"A little boring, I guess," she said. "Where is everybody? This place feels like a ghost town."

Sans gave a brief laugh. "Andy should be here any second now."

A moment later, Ramsay escorted a furious-looking Andy into the room. "What the hell did you do with her, you bastard?" he shouted at Sans.

He remained calm and put up his hand. "Please, take a seat."

Ramsay brought him over to the chair next to Chang, then walked around behind Sans to sit across from her.

Sans sighed and seemed to relax his shoulders. "Now that we're all here, let's enjoy dinner."

"Where the hell is Sydney?" Andy said.

Chang glanced at Sans. "Billy, what's going on?"

He put up his hand towards her. "You will all have your answers in good time. But first, let's eat."

A servant brought out a plate of Chapati bread for the table and returned with plates of *nyoma choma* chicken kebabs for each of them. They ate in silence. Chang saw Andy glaring at Sans repeatedly, but the man at the head of the table seemed perfectly calm, as if all was right with the world.

Sans waited until they had all finished, then clapped his hands together. "I believe a friend is waiting for us. Let's pay them a visit, shall we?" He stood up and led them to the front door, Ramsay following closely behind. Chang wondered what was going on. They marched out onto the patio and hung a left to the path through the woods.

"You'll finally get to visit the rest of the labs, Ellie. Our dear friend Richard was just *dying* to see them," he said with disdain. His mood seemed to have become embittered on the walk over.

Finally, they entered the building and Sans took them to the rear, where there were a stairwell and an elevator. "Let's exercise, shall we?" he said, swiftly descending the steps.

Chang and Andy waited at the top for a moment. She had a strange feeling about this, but Ramsay nudged her forward. When they finally reached the bottom, she saw that it was much darker down here and the lights cast a strange blue glow. They turned a corner and continued down a long hallway with some pipes running along the walls that she guessed were for gas. Everything else was metallic gray. It gave her an eerie vibe as they followed Sans around another corner and into a rocky cavern.

"I never pictured you as one for theatrics, Billy," she said, glancing around.

He shrugged. "Times change." He strolled off to the left, where she could see several barred cells along the wall.

She peered closer at the one nearest to her. It seemed like there was something in there, a dark shape–

A thing with gnashing teeth and red eyes lunged for the gate, snarling angrily and spewing saliva.

Chang reeled back and heard Sans chuckling. She shot him an angry glance. "What the *fuck* is that?!"

He smiled. "The results I promised the board. The base

was a lion, but through the wonders of gene therapy I've enhanced it beyond its natural abilities. It's about to be obsolete though, the latest version is far more advanced."

A second red-eyed beast appeared in the next cell over, but Sans calmly walked to the third and gestured for them to come closer. "See for yourself."

Slowly, she and Andy walked over. It was dark in the cage, but she could see something huddled at the back. It had a human shape. A head raised towards them and Chang saw golden eyes looking at her out of the darkness.

"Don't be shy, everyone wants to see you," Sans addressed the creature.

The eyes didn't move.

Sans sighed. "Insecurity; it's a terrible thing." He turned to Ramsay. "She must be starving, let's give her something."

Ramsay silently disappeared down another hallway and came back a minute later wearing gloves and holding a fat, white rat in his hands. Chang watched as he slid a latch and a small opening appeared, which he then shoved the animal through.

Before the rodent could even try and squeeze back through the bars, the creature pounced into view with lightning speed. It caught the tiny animal with its bare hands and sank its sharp teeth into the rat's neck, blood drizzling down onto the floor.

Chang covered her mouth. Even with the leopard-like fur, the creature's face and sandy blonde hair were unmistakable.

It was Sydney.

The girl paused from eating and raised her head up, blood and bits of raw meat dripping from her jaws. She glanced between all of them and looked ashamed, then retreated to the back of the cell to continue her meal.

"What the hell did you do to her?!" Andy hissed.

"The same thing I'm going to do to you if you don't shut up," Sans said without looking at him. He strode forward and looked into Sydney's prison. "Tomorrow, there will be no more troublesome behavior – only compliance, or I'll start your friend here on the virus. I'm going to let you loose into the reserve and you'll have a whole day's head-start. You'll be injected with a shocker implant that won't let you get past any of the electromagnetic boundaries. I will start hunting you at night and if you can survive for a week, I'll switch to tranquilizers and be able to re-use you. It is in your interest to provide me with the most thrilling sport of my life, or I may feel compelled to replace you with your friend." He pressed his face against the bars. "Do you understand?"

At the back of the cell, a pair of golden eyes glared back at him. Silence.

He smiled. "Good." He turned back to his guests, both of whom were petrified. "Let's head back to the lodge, shall we?"

Suddenly, Andy rushed forward and gave Sans a strong right hook across the jaw. Ramsay was upon him in a second, throwing him to the ground. Chang tried to pull him away, but Ramsay smacked her off and began kicking Andy as he lay on the cavern floor.

She regained her bearing and ran forward again, but this time Sans held her back. Chang saw a wild gleam in his eye, snarling with pleasure as he watched his assailant take a beating. She struggled to break free, but he suddenly yelled: "Stop!"

Ramsay stepped back. Andy was doubled over on the ground.

Sans let go of Chang and walked closer. "Try that again, and I'll feed you to the hybrids right now."

"Don't!" came a voice. They all turned to see Sydney at the bars, a look of worry on her face.

"Oh look," Sans said. "It speaks."

Three technicians had come out. One roughly grabbed Chang's arm and the others hauled Andy to his feet. There was blood dripping from his nose.

Sans began walking back the way they came. "Let's get the hell out of here," he called behind him. "I need a bloody drink."

TRUTH

The sun was just reaching the horizon when Chang walked out onto the balcony, her polo shirt-clad escort right by her side. Sans was sitting in a chair, flipping through a copy of Capstick's *The African Adventurers*, a bottle of Tusker by his side. He appeared absorbed in what he was reading, then noticed she was there and raised his head. A warm smile came to his face.

"Lovely view, isn't it?" he said.

Chang nodded. "Spectacular," she said quietly.

"I like to come out here and enjoy it from time to time. It's best when there's a cool br–"

"How'd you do it?" she blurted.

Sans smiled. "Lentiviral gene therapy. It's the future."

"I mean how did you create the virus? How did you get it to do that to her?"

"Well first, I removed the parts of the strain that caused illness and replaced it with, in her case, *Panthera pardus pardus* DNA. It's more complicated in practice, but that's the basic gist of it." He almost made it sound simple. "I call it the Moreau virus. Catchy, don't you think?"

"But why?"

"Why what?"

"Why'd you do what you did to her?"

He laughed. "You think I turned her into a monster."

"The only monster I've seen today is you." Her eyes were cold as stones.

Sans smirked and looked back at his book. "On hunting, Capstick once said: 'That is man against himself, the last and purest of the challenges that made us men, not animals.'"

"He also said: 'There are no Great White Hunters. Mediocre, at best.'"

"Well, if Mr. Capstick could see what I've done here, I'd like to think he'd reconsider."

"I doubt it. You're a disgrace to the entire sport."

Sans glared at her for a moment. "You're not the first to misunderstand me and you won't be the last." He went back to reading.

After a moment, Chang clenched her fists, exhaled, and said, "I'm sorry."

He looked up, confused.

"I'm sorry," she continued. "I knew how much Jane's death affected you, but I thought you needed space, not help. I should've been there for you more and instead–"

"Oh for fuck's sake," he said, getting up and walking off to the edge of the balcony. After a moment, he turned around, looking angrier than before. "You know what? I really hate people like you, who come in at the end after someone's had issues and think a few damn words are gonna make a difference. My whole life, I've had to find my own support and it got me this far. Aside from my parents, there have only been two people who actually *helped* me: my speech therapist and my wife. The first was paid to do so, and the other is dead." He lisped the word *first* but seemed not to notice.

Chang was silent. She looked off beyond the savanna to the west. The sun was gone now and the orange blur on the horizon was receding from the darkening sky. "They'll find out," she said, finally.

"Who? Are you going to run back to the board, to the authorities? Do you honestly think I'd be stupid enough to let you leave?"

"Someone will find out, eventually."

"How, Ellie? You and Andy are stuck here. I reported you dead in a safari accident along with everyone else."

Her heart skipped a beat. "When?"

"Last Thursday."

She was quiet for a moment, her mind racing. "Are you going to kill me?"

He paused. "That depends on how this conversation ends." Chang felt her muscles tense up. Sans smiled. "I'd advise you to choose your words very carefully from now on."

She swallowed. "After the interns are dead, you're going to need new people."

"That's right."

"You can't keep luring college students here."

"Oh no, of course not. They're just prototypes, test runs. Long term, I have something far superior planned."

She wondered, if she elbowed the man beside her in the throat, how long it would take her to run down the stairs, out the back door, and up to the air field. Could she get the plane started in time? No, that was ridiculous. His other men would catch her before she'd made it out of the lodge.

"And what's that?"

Sans smiled, clearly delighting in finally being able to tell someone all this. "I'm going to arrange for the greatest big-game hunters in the world to be kidnapped and brought here. Then I'll use the Moreau virus on them, both the perfected versions of the current strains and new ones Graves and I are devising. *That* will be the ultimate sport: the finest wits in this game armed with the deadliest natural attributes."

"So it's going to continue on forever, then? Or are you just doing all of this until you can create something that finally kills you because you can't do it yourself?"

His eyes narrowed. "I've finally found my purpose, Ellie. I'm enjoying life for the first time in years."

"But you're hurting other people."

Sans calmly shook his head. "You just don't understand. I wouldn't expect you to, anyway."

At that moment, everything changed. She thought back to when she first met him, a shy guy in one of her Stanford MBA classes. She'd always been good at making friends with introverts. In undergrad, one of her friends had accused her of taking the socially awkward under her wing as "charity cases". The truth was, she'd been a pariah in middle school and no one ever extended special courtesy to her. Starting in high school, she'd decided to always give people like that a chance and it had continued ever since.

Once his shell was broken, Sans proved to be a charmingly pleasant acquaintance. They'd become good friends and as the years went by she'd found herself being incorporated more into his social network, rather than the other way around. They'd kept in touch even as they worked in different fields; him in Big Pharma and her as a Silicon Valley venture capitalist. Over time, he developed much more confidence through success and tapped into his inner ability to lead and create a vision for the future.

That was what had inspired John Giger, the CEO of the company following Gerard Sans's death, to name Billy as his successor in 2003. He'd immediately begun making changes, moving the headquarters to America and shifting SansCorp's focus from developing medicines towards genetic research and engineering. He'd eventually brought her in as the new CFO and told her his grand vision for the future of biotech. He'd been far more ambitious then.

That Billy was gone.

Now he was consumed solely by a hobby, pouring his energy and intellect into something that, even if she managed to escape this place, Chang doubted anyone sane would ever believe.

"What would Jane think?"

Anger suddenly flashed through his eyes. "Leave her out of this."

"Answer me. What would she think?"

He stormed towards her, his face turning red as he spoke rapidly. "She would've understood, goddammit! She would've understood because I would have explained and she would've seen things my way, okay?" There was the lisp again, on *seen*.

Chang glanced at the sweatband around his wrist. Today it was purple. A thought came to mind. She almost stopped herself from saying it. Almost.

"It would've been better if she never found you that night."

Before she even knew what was happening, he had his hands around her throat and she was falling down, down to the hard wood floor. She closed her eyes and braced herself for the impact. When she opened them, Sans was gazing down at her with pure hatred. His grip continued to tighten and she realized he meant to kill her.

The staff member was simply standing by in her

peripheral vision. No one was going to help. She tugged at Sans's arms but they didn't budge. Her lungs were burning. She punched upward, connecting with one of his cheekbones. He shook his head and squeezed harder, his face contorting. His expression seemed almost inhuman.

She struggled, she thrashed, she punched again, she dug her nails into the skin of his hands. He let up for a split second, and she started to wriggle free. He slammed her back against the wood multiple times. Blackness crept around the edges of her eyes. She opened her mouth, trying to take in any air that she could.

Suddenly, the grasp his hands held around her neck loosened. Chang gasped for breath, feeling the glorious sensation of air entering her lungs. Sans stood up, pulling himself together. He looked exhausted, but angry.

"I'm going to keep you around," he said, pointing his finger down at her, "just so that I can prove you wrong. When you start to bore me, I'll leave you to the animals."

He walked off. Slowly, she sat up and coughed, still breathing heavily. The worker stepped closer and silently stood over her, waiting to take her back to her room where she wouldn't be let out without supervision.

As she prepared to stand up, her heart still pounding, she looked off at the horizon and saw the last glimpses of orange were gone.

Night had descended on the Serengeti.

OPTIONS

Sydney huddled in the darkness at the back of her cell. The distant dripping of water became ever more noticeable in her ears, which, as far as she could tell, hadn't started morphing into a cat's yet. Everything hurt and she was still hungry, but her mind was fixated on other things.

Tomorrow, she was going to be hunted for sport. She would have a week to evade Sans before he agreed to continue his pursuit with non-lethal force. She could hide from him on the reserve forever and the implant would still prevent her escape. She had thought of tearing it out, but she didn't know where they would put it. Sans or Graves would have thought that through.

She didn't know why he was holding Chang and Andy over her like that. They were all as good as dead now, anyway. She was just postponing their suffering by agreeing to his rules.

Gradually, she realized that Sans had everything under control and could decide people's fates on a whim, depending on his mood.

Or really, he *thought* he had everything under control.

His hubris was her opening. Sans was getting cocky, and when people got cocky they were likely to overlook certain things. Tonight was her last chance before they put the implant in. She wouldn't be able to get back into the lodge perimeter after that, and it didn't look like she'd be able to infiltrate the labs through the cave unless she wanted to end up like Jones.

So she had to do something and she had to do it now.

There was no clock down here, so she didn't know what time it was. The cavern had the same dark gloom all hours of the day and night, so the only frame of reference she had was when Sans had brought the others to see her. That had been many hours ago, but she was sure it was now sometime very early in the morning. She assumed that she only had a few hours to work with.

Slowly, she got up and walked over to the bars. The keypad was out of sight, but she knew where it was and she could probably reach her arm through enough to get to it. Still, she didn't know the code and there was no way of getting it.

Graves and the technicians hadn't run any more tests on her and she knew that when they came for her next, it would be for the implant. Besides, there were always too many of them. She would be overwhelmed, even with her claws. It just took one well-placed injection to sedate her and then she was entirely at their mercy. She sat down and looked around the enclosed space, thinking.

All that was left of the rat earlier was a few bones scattered on the floor.

Then she thought of an idea.

Around twenty minutes later, two technicians entered the cavern.

They were heading towards the computer lab down the operating room corridor when one of them stopped.

"Do you hear that?" he said.

The other listened. A strange, guttural noise was coming from one of the cages, the one with the girl – or whatever the hell she was now.

They rushed over to the cell. Behind the bars, Sydney was doubled over and clutching her throat. She glanced up towards them and the look in her eyes pleaded for help.

"Shit," the first man said, sliding over to the keypad and punching in the code. "She's choking on the rat bones."

"Didn't anybody clean that up?" the other asked.

"We only clean the cages once a week," the first technician said as the gate slid open. He ran over to Sydney, then stopped before getting too close.

"What are you waiting for?" the second asked.

"I mean, she's dangerous–"

"If she dies on our watch, Dr. Sans will feed us to the others."

"Fuck," the man said, bending down to Sydney–

She shot up and slammed him back against the wall with as much force as she could muster, his skull cracking against the rock.

"Oh shit," the second tech said, diving for the keypad.

Thinking quickly, Sydney pushed the dazed man into the opening as the titanium gate shot across. He landed on his side and the metal connected with his chest, crushing his ribs inward. Blood spurted from his mouth and he began to twitch, but he was heavyset enough that there was still nearly a foot gap left open.

The other technician's eyes went wide with horror and he ran off back the way he came screaming, "Security! Help!"

She had to move quickly; there wouldn't be much time before more came. Holding her breath, she squeezed herself through the opening and fell to the ground. She scrambled back to her feet and moved towards the other hallway, looking back over her shoulder. There were voices approaching from the way the tech ran off.

Sydney entered the corridor and ran to the door on the right, opening it to find the lab pitch black save for the glow of computer screens. Her eyes adjusted to the dark much faster now and she dove under a desk beside the door and waited, her heart pounding.

Several minutes passed.

She slowly peered out from her cover to look out the hallway window, but no one was visible. She could hear voices coming from the cavern. They would know she had to have come this way, and other than the lab there were only the two operating rooms.

It wouldn't take long for them to find her.

She'd positioned herself near the door so that if they went to the back of the room, she'd have a chance at escape. But she didn't know how many were out there. If one of them remained outside the door, she could take them. After all, she'd handled that technician.

I killed him, she thought, the horrific realization just dawning on her. Her hands started trembling for a moment, but she took a breath and clenched her fists. *Get it together*. She thought the man had looked familiar, but couldn't quite place his face. It took her a moment to realize that when she'd seen him before, he'd been wearing a medical mask and had been seated behind the monitors during the electroshock session.

She shivered at the memory. It was time to get the hell out of here. Just as she started to crawl for the door, it swung open and a tall Afrikaner man entered, swinging around a Glock pistol in one hand and aiming a flashlight with the other. She vaguely remembered him as the driver of the other SUV on the first day's safari.

"Come out, come out, pretty kitty," he muttered, walking past where she hid towards the rows of computers on tables in the center of the room. "Time to go back to bed."

She briefly glanced out from under the desk and saw the nervous second technician from earlier in the hall. So, it was just two of them right now. Most of the others must've been upstairs or off shift. And the tech wasn't armed.

A radio on the driver's belt crackled. "Kobus, what's your status?"

"I've got a small situation down in the cave. Cartwright is dead, but don't worry – I'm on it."

"That doesn't sound like a small situation–"

"I said *I'm on it*, okay?"

She wondered if she should move now, take out the tech in the hallway, then make a break for it. No, she didn't know how good a shot Kobus was. She needed to–

He swung the light onto her. "There you are! Don't move!"

She dove out of the way and crawled through the dark past one of the rows of computers. Kobus tried to run around the back, but she rolled under the table to other side.

"What the hell are you doing?" she heard the tech ask from the door. She recognized his voice as the American who tried to sedate her the night before.

"I train the gun on her, you ready the syringe," he said.

"Yeah," the American said. "But how the hell do you think you're gonna–"

Sydney made her move. She leapt out at Kobus, but he had better reflexes than she'd anticipated. He hit her forehead with the flashlight so hard she nearly blacked out. The next thing she knew, she was careening backward and toppling over a table, knocking several flat-screen monitors off the edge. They smashed on the floor around her as her body hit the hard surface.

"What the fuck are you doing?!" the American screamed. "Do you know how much those cost?"

"Shut up and get over here, Marcus," Kobus said.

Everything hurt. She heard footsteps and saw him coming closer, shining the beam directly at her face. She raised a hand to shield her eyes from the light and could make out the barrel of the Glock aimed down at her. Marcus was making his way around the other side.

"Hurry, before she tries anything again," Kobus told him.

She groaned, rubbing her forehead. She hoped she didn't have a concussion.

Marcus crouched beside her and readied the syringe. She quickly glanced between him and the gun. *They won't shoot me. Sans would kill them.*

Marcus quickly jabbed the needle towards her neck–

She grabbed his hand, pulled it in front of her face, and bit down on his wrist in a fluid motion. He screamed as her teeth reached the bone and Kobus swept down like a bird of prey to pin her down, pressing both of her arms against the floor.

Marcus reeled back and clutched his wound as the syringe tumbled away.

"Get back here!" Kobus hissed. The flashlight pointed away and the gun was still in his hand, aimed away from her head as he applied pressure to keep her down.

Angrily, she jerked her shoulders as hard as she could and her right arm came free just long enough for her to reach up and stick her clawed thumb into Kobus's left eye. He howled in pain as she pushed deeper into the socket, thick drops of blood raining down on her. The gun and flashlight scattered away across the floor as she got to her feet and pulled her hand away.

Kobus was on his knees, clutching his face. Channeling her rage, she grabbed him by the back of his head and smashed his face against the side of the nearest table. His limp body slid to the floor, unmoving. Before she could figure out if he was dead or merely unconscious, she heard a door closing and saw Marcus fleeing down the corridor through the window.

Turning, she made out the shape of the pistol lying on the darkened floor, grabbed it, and ran to the exit. Her own speed surprised her as she flung open the door and gave chase to the running technician, who was now out into the cavern.

"Freeze!" she yelled after him. He didn't listen. She fired the gun.

Marcus stumbled to the ground and turned around, arms outstretched. He looked terrified as she came out into the high-ceilinged space and trained the weapon on him. She didn't consider herself a good shot, but he didn't know that.

"Please," he pleaded, getting to his feet. "You don't understand. Dr. Sans...he's a visionary. What he's done with you is nothing short of remarkable–"

"Shut. The fuck. Up," Sydney said, moving closer. She could definitely hit him at this range. From the hallway that led back to the upper floors, she could hear several more footsteps approaching. They sounded far off, thundering down flights of stairs. Her eyes darted over to the gate about twenty feet away, with the big heavy door that led to the rest of the cave system.

She looked back at Marcus. "You know the code?"

"Yes."

"Open it."

"I can't let those things out. They'll kill us all!"

"You think I won't?" she said.

Marcus slowly got up and started walking over to the gate. He was about to punch something in on the keypad, then turned back to her. "This is a very bad idea."

"Add it to the list." She watched as he punched in the code. The door clicked open. "Block it with your shoe."

Marcus slipped off his loafer, pulled the door open slightly, and wedged it in. Sydney scanned the darkness for any sign of red eyes or a moving shape. Nothing. Marcus glanced over at the hallway, shaking with terror. He was clearly hoping the cavalry would save him, and by the sound of it, they were right around the corner. She started to back up.

He looked at her. "This isn't going to end well for–"

A massive creature burst out of the door, lunging forward with sharp claws extended and horrifying teeth barred. Its eyes were the color of blood.

BREAKOUT

Marcus screamed and darted for the safety of the corridor. The monster was upon him in an instant, knocking him to the ground and biting through his vertebrae with a bone-chilling *snap*. Sydney backed towards the computer lab and operating rooms as quickly as she could, never taking her eyes off the feeding predator.

Suddenly, it turned its head toward her and growled. Now that she had a full view of the thing, it was even more terrifying. It was at least eight feet long and didn't have a mane, so it was probably female. Its mangy beige fur was covered with hyena spots and the claws appeared to be over two inches long. Viscera clung to its teeth and crimson saliva drooled onto the cave floor as it pawed its way closer.

If she broke into a run, it would leap for her. If she kept backing up, it would gain on her. She could shoot it, but if she missed the head she risked just pissing it off. She was wondering how quickly she could sprint for the nearest operating room door when two of Sans's men burst in with pistols and opened fire at the creature.

One bullet grazed its back, and the hybrid angrily turned and moved in their direction with frightening speed. The men backed around the corner, the sounds of their gunfire receding with them as the beast gave pursuit. It disappeared after them and she heard screaming. The gunfire stopped.

A second one smashed the door open again and she realized the shoe was still in place. She pressed her back against the rocky wall. The thing looked between her and where the screams were coming from. She gripped the pistol at her side, this time ready to fire.

There was a burst of gunfire and a dog-like yelp. The hybrid immediately bounded in that direction. There were more gunshots and suddenly the sound of something bursting and a rushing noise that sounded like gas escaping.

Then there was an explosion.

The *bang* resounded all around the cavern and Sydney covered her ears. Her improved hearing made her more susceptible to loud noises and she waited a moment to gather her bearings while the ringing subsided.

Flames were licking around the corner of the hallway and an alarm was blaring. The limp figure of a man lay just in her line of sight. She stumbled closer to get a better look when she saw him start to get up. He put a hand to his head, then turned towards her.

It was Ramsay.

He shot her a look that could kill and drew his revolver, entering the cavern. She was beginning to take larger steps backwards as he raised the gun toward her.

"I told Dr. Sans you were a problem. Told him you proved

the leopard virus worked and that we should just move onto the boy, but no. He was convinced. I never doubt Dr. Sans, but this time I'm afraid I'm taking matters into my own hands."

He fired. Sydney ducked, but in the process her Glock slipped from her fingers. Before she could pick it up, he shot another round and it whizzed by her close enough for her to hear it. She took off into the corridor and he fired a third shot, the bullet cracking the computer lab window She made it to the end of the hall just as he reappeared.

Sydney swung the second operating room's door open and slammed it behind her before he could fire again, frantically checking for a lock.

There wasn't one. She moved a table beside her in front of the door, even though she knew it would barely slow him down. Then she turned around to look for a place to hide and gasped.

Brandon was lying on the operating table, his eyelids closed over. A monitor was showing his heart rate constant at 70 beats per minute. He was clad only in blue latex medical shorts but there were bandages all over his torso and around his head. He possessed more animalistic features than she did, with a thicker coat of fur and a much bulkier muscle mass. The talons on the ends of his fingers were thicker and sharper than hers.

Without thinking, she ran up to him and swiftly pulled the IV tube out of his arm.

His eyelids fluttered just as Ramsay kicked the door open, knocking the blockade a few feet back. She hid behind the operating table as his second kick dislodged her barrier entirely and her pursuer came into the room.

She expected him to wait there for a moment, taunting her to come out and that there was no escape like they always said in movies. But instead, he silently started around the operating table towards her. She quietly scurried to the other side, trying to keep low.

It was too little, too late. He swung the firearm over Brandon's body and aimed for her skull. Sydney's eyes went wide and she swiftly ducked just as a deafening gunshot resounded in her ears and the bullet passed less than an inch over her head.

She collapsed to the floor, the ringing unbearable. *Get up*, she told herself. *Get up now*.

There was a commotion on the table above and she heard Ramsay cry out. Scurrying for the door, she looked back to see Brandon digging his claws into the man's gun-wielding arm and sinking his teeth into his bicep.

Not wasting a second, Sydney hauled the door open and dashed out into the hallway. She only got about halfway back to the cavern before she heard glass breaking behind her and threw her head over her shoulder to see Ramsay tumbling to the gray floor amongst scores of shards.

The Brandon-thing pounced out from the room onto him and she found herself stopping to watch in horrified fascination as it dug its talons through Ramsay's abdomen. The man screamed, his eyes wide in terror, as the bestial hybrid ripped his intestines out and brought them to its mouth.

Sydney felt sick to her stomach, stumbling backwards. Smoke was wafting into her nostrils from somewhere behind her, but her attention was transfixed on the writhing figure of Ramsay as he was eaten alive. Blood poured from his mouth as he reached back towards her, a look of hopelessness etched on his face. The creature that had been Brandon voraciously tore its head away from the entrails to rip off a bite, then came back for more, its face smeared with crimson.

She snapped out of her trance and turned around, running towards the cavern as acrid smoke filled her nose. She coughed as she stumbled out of the man-made hallway and into the natural space. The path to the stairs was now a raging inferno of flames. Dread filled her as she realized there was only one other way out.

The cave.

The shoe was still functioning as a doorstop, though it'd been shifted slightly. If she was going in there, she was going to need more than her claws. She looked around on the cavern floor for the Glock, but it was black and so was the ground. As she tried retracing her steps, her foot kicked something on the cave floor and she heard it scatter away across the rocky surface.

Sydney got down on her hands and knees, hearing the Brandon-thing roar somewhere behind her. It sounded like a hoarse, demented version of a lion. Hurrying her pace, she swept her hand along the ground and her fingertips found the barrel. She scooped the pistol up and got to her feet, coughing. The smoke was almost unbearable.

She stumbled across the cavern to the door and grasped the handle, aiming the Glock into the dark in case there were any more hybrids. She didn't see any. Keeping her gun at the ready, she eased forward into the blackness and accidentally knocked the shoe out of place.

The titanium door slammed shut behind her.

There was no going back now.

She coughed and continued into the cave, letting her eyes adjust as she walked. The tunnel curved to her left and the blueish glow of the cavern lights faded as she rounded the bend. Sydney kept close to the side, her whole body tense and alert.

The familiar dripping noise grew louder, echoing from a distant point ahead. The ceiling appeared to be only ten feet or so here and the ground was much more jagged; she had to be careful not to slip and break her ankle.

The place made her think of Kitum Cave in Kenya's Mount Elgon National Park. It was where two visitors had contracted the Marburg virus in the 1980s, a sickness that causes one's internal organs to melt from the inside out. It was currently believed to be contracted by inhaling dust from bat guano.

She tried to put the thought out of her mind.

The ground was beginning to slope upward beneath her feet. There was a big, black empty space coming up ahead. She realized it was another cavern and there appeared to be some kind of ledge she needed to climb.

Sydney felt her hand along it and realized it was barely a foot shorter than she was. She lay the gun on the next level and hauled herself up, but as her waist cleared the landing she heard a guttural growl.

Two red eyes locked onto her from twenty feet away. The creature was a dark outline in her vision, a black shadow ready to pounce. Without taking her eyes off it, Sydney carefully felt for the gun beside her, her left elbow keeping her propped up on the ledge. She felt her index finger curl around the trigger as her palm found the grip.

The monster moved for her, red pupils gliding through the dark with frightening speed. She ducked down just as it leapt over the ledge, the pistol going off in an upward direction.

The thing yelped and landed a few feet away, twisting and contorting itself on the ground, writhing its way towards her. Frightened, she fired again. She saw the beast's razor-sharp fangs in the flash, its jaws agape. When she squeezed the trigger a third time, it was even closer. The ferocity in its monstrous eyes seared their way into her mind.

She fired again, and again, and again. On the last shot, she briefly glimpsed the hybrid's skullcap exploding open, then it was gone.

All was quiet. The steady dripping noise returned.

She sat breathing heavily against the ledge for a few moments, her wrist sore from the recoil. Then she got up and peered over it. Nothing was there. Swiftly, she pulled herself up and ran forward, keeping the gun at her side in case anything jumped out at the last second.

The ground sloped upward gently and to the right, and she saw with great relief that she was approaching the mouth of the cave. She ran out into the warm night and almost collapsed out of sheer happiness. The sky was beginning to lighten, which meant it had to be after six in the morning.

An enormous *boom* resounded somewhere off to her right, and she ran around the rock formation to see a fireball amongst the trees to the right of the lodge, which still had its lights on about half a mile away.

The main lab building had exploded. Somehow the fire had reached the upper levels or the gas leak had spread. Regardless, it was gone now.

Then, it hit her. Most of Sans's research had been in there. All the data on gene therapy, the hybrids… *Any chance for a cure*, she realized.

She turned and slammed her fist against the rocky surface beside her. It hurt and she gritted her teeth. Something else dawned on her: all the electromagnetic controls had been located in that building. They might be down, which meant she wouldn't be safe even after she got back inside the perimeter until daybreak.

Keeping the Glock clutched firmly in her hand, she started making her way toward the lodge.

LODGE

Chang's eyes shot open. She sat up and looked around her darkened room; the clock on her nightstand glowed 6:34 in red digits. Rubbing her temple, she went over to the window and pulled back the curtain. It was just before sunrise and the sky looked clear save for a few clouds. There was no sign of a storm.

Then that couldn't have been thunder, she thought.

She quickly changed into a t-shirt, khaki shorts, and boots and opened her bedroom door. To her surprise, there wasn't a guard on duty outside like there had been earlier. She glanced down the hallway towards Andy's room. Nobody was there either.

Chang immediately knew then that, regardless of what was happening, this was her chance. Inching down the hall to the landing, she saw that Sans's door had been left open. She glanced down the stairs to the foyer and saw no one.

Walking faster now, she headed down the west hall to Andy's room and knocked on the door. Groggily, he opened it. "What's going on?"

"Get dressed. We're leaving."

"Twist my arm," he said, disappearing.

Chang looked back down the hallway to make sure no one was coming. There were no sounds from downstairs. If they could just slip away through the back door out the library, they could make a break for the airstrip. It'd been nearly two years since she last flew a plane, but she knew the Cessna 208. It might be a little bumpy, but they had to get out of here.

She didn't know what they could do about Sydney, however. It was too much to risk it trying to break her out of the labs. If she escaped with Andy, Sans would only have one human-hybrid to hunt so he'd keep her alive longer until she could alert the authorities–

Two shots rang out somewhere outside. She held her breath, listening very carefully. They hadn't sounded far off.

Then came a human scream.

"Andy, hurry up," she hissed through the opening in the door.

He appeared a second later, a backpack slung over his shoulder. "Let's go."

They arrived at the top of the stairs and Chang motioned for him to hold up. She peered down into the foyer and still heard no one.

"Should we run for it?" Andy whispered. "We're going to the plane, right?"

"Yes, but I think they're trying to contain something outside."

"That should keep them distracted."

"But we don't to attract *its* attention by running," she said.

Together, they slowly descended the steps, trying not to

make too much noise. *To hell with it*, Chang thought. She began walking at a normal pace and reached the bottom of the stairs, then turned and saw a figure seated in the dining room.

It was Graves. A pistol lay at her side. "Don't make me use this," she said, looking it over. "I'm a better shot than you might think."

"What's going on?" Chang asked, wondering if she was bluffing.

"The laboratories just exploded. Dr. Sans is out with the others trying to get it sorted out."

There were more gunshots and another scream from outside.

"Sounds like they're doing a bloody good job of it," Andy said.

Graves smirked and stood up, keeping one hand rested atop the gun. "Dr. Sans is the finest hunter history has ever seen. Even if a few of the specimens have escaped, they will be swiftly dealt with. The others are who *I'm* worried about."

She gazed off out the window and Chang seized her chance. She grabbed Andy by the arm and began running towards the back of the house and the library—

When suddenly Fatou stepped around the corner, holding a kitchen knife. The two of them started to back up as Graves walked out behind them, aiming the pistol at Chang's head.

"You see?" The red-haired woman smirked. "Escape is pointless. The emitters are down and those things will tear you to pieces. Besides, where would you go?" Chang said nothing. "Oh, you're going to try to fly the *plane*. Well, good luck with that."

"I got my pilot's license at seventeen, you bitch."

Graves just smiled smugly. "Do you really think anyone would believe you? All the evidence just went up in flames."

"You people are mental," Andy said.

"Your profile said you were intelligent, but clearly you

can't comprehend Dr. Sans's genius."

"Oh, we can comprehend it," Chang said. Fatou was right behind her. If she pulled anything, they'd be more likely to injure or even kill her than Andy. She was only alive for Sans's amusement at this point, whereas if Sydney had died in the explosion he was now of prime importance to them. "You took technology meant to save lives and twisted it for sadistic purposes. People like you are why science gets a bad rap."

"Science doesn't need good publicity," Graves stated calmly. "It is a tool for advancement; it always has been and it always will be. And advancement takes many forms."

A radio crackled on her belt. "Lodge, come in. This is Banners. I repeat: lodge, come in."

Without taking her aim or her eyes off Chang, she held it up. "This is Lodge, Graves speaking. What's the situation?"

The man's voice on the other end sounded desperate. "They're everywhere. We've killed at least four of them and some must've died in the explosion, but there's still a fair number left."

"What happened to the labs?" she asked.

"Venter went in. There was a fire coming up from the basement. One of the things attacked him and he fired. It must've set off some gas leak or something. I barely got out. My ears are still ringing."

"Where's Ramsay?"

"He went to the lower level earlier, didn't come out. He must be dead."

"How many are left?"

"I think just Dr. Sans and myself. I don't know where he is."

"He's doing what he does best," Graves said. "It's almost dawn and they'll retreat to the cave soon. Then we can sort out this mess with Dr. Sans. You better get back here."

"Understood. I'm on my way. Should be there in five,

over."

"Copy that," Graves said. She slowly lowered the radio, her icy gaze still fixed on Chang. "Fatou, I think it's time we had some morning coffee."

"Agreed," he said.

Graves stepped aside and motioned for them to walk ahead. The four of them went to the dining room. "Take a seat," she said. Chang and Andy reluctantly sat down while Graves did so across the table, keeping the gun trained in the space between them.

"How do you like your coffee?" Graves asked.

"I don't drink it," Chang replied.

"I only have fair trade with Madagascar vanilla. If the creamer isn't just right, I send it back," Andy said.

Graves smiled in contempt. "I wish Dr. Sans had decided to hunt you first."

"But then I wouldn't get to experience your warm personality every day."

The radio crackled again. "This is Graves. What is it?"

Static.

Shared confusion hung in the air between them, then: "…need help! Now!"

"Banners, where are you?" Graves asked.

"Oh Jesus, it's right–"

Static again, followed by garbled noises, then nothing.

"Fatou," she called. "Scratch the coffee." He came back out. "How safe are we in here?"

"Not very."

"That's what I feared." She stood up and motioned with the gun. "We're going back upstairs to Dr. Sans's office. It's the most secure room. Move!"

They moved out into the foyer and started up the stairs when a violent knock came from the door. They turned around.

The knock came again. And again.

"Fatou, open it. It's Banners."

Cautiously, he edged down the stairs and slowly reached for the handle. Graves kept her gun aimed at the door as Chang and Andy slowly backed further up past her.

The door opened with a creak. Fatou peered outside and Chang could see that the sky was much brighter now, an orange glow appearing along the horizon. The seconds passed slowly as he looked in both directions, then threw his head back towards Graves.

"He's not out—"

Abruptly, he heard something and rushed to shut the door just as one of the hybrids appeared, viciously barging its way through. Fatou turned and ran to the base of the stairs while Graves screamed and pulled the trigger.

Her aim, Chang realized, wasn't so great after all. A red spot appeared on the chef's white uniform, square in his chest. He toppled back down to the floor while the beast ignored him entirely and started up the steps after them. Chang and Andy were already sprinting to the top of the landing and hurtling towards Sans's open door.

Just as they slipped inside, she heard a horrible shriek and spun around to see that the hybrid had tackled Graves near the top of the stairs. It wrapped its jaws around the base of her neck. Her face contorted in pain, her mouth stretching agape. Then, with the ghastly sound of vertebral dislodgement, the creature jerked its head upwards and Graves's head tore away from her body, a bloody spray cascading in all directions—

Chang slammed the big door shut, locked it, and leaned against the wall, hyperventilating.

ESCAPE

Sydney stayed close to the treeline as she went, crouching and occasionally pausing between each trunk. She had heard gunfire not long ago, and screaming, but that all seemed to be concentrated near the burning wreck of the veterinary labs. Nevertheless, she kept her pistol at the ready.

The lodge was just ahead; it had taken her nearly twenty minutes to get here from the cave and the sun was now rising above the savanna to the east. Sans had to have Andy and Chang held inside, if he hadn't already done something to them...

She tried to ignore the grumbling in her stomach, but it wasn't working. All she'd had to eat in the past twenty-four hours was a rat.

Focus, she told herself. Most of Sans's men would be out in the forest dealing with the escaped hybrids. Chang and Andy would be comparatively low priorities, so there were probably only one or two people left inside to watch them. She wasn't sure how many rounds were still in the Glock, but she knew they held seventeen bullets and she hadn't fired half of those yet. Hopefully, this would be quick and they could get to the plane and bail the fuck out of here.

She walked out onto the front patio by the pool and saw the door was wide open. Keeping close to the side of the building, she inched forward and took a deep breath. Then she entered the lodge, gun first.

Fatou was lying on his back, the front of his shirt soaked with the blood of a gunshot wound. Sydney immediately had a glimmer of hope that Andy or Chang had been responsible during some kind of escape, but as her eyes traveled up the stairs she had to cover her mouth in shock.

Graves's severed head lay on a step. Her skin was ghostly pale, having been drained of blood. The perpetrator appeared at the edge of the second-floor landing, gore smeared across its monstrous mouth.

Immediately, Sydney pulled the door shut and looked around. The pillars under the balcony were wooden; could she climb that? *Only one way to find out.*

She sprinted as fast as she could across the pool deck, hearing the animal repeatedly smash itself against the wood. Finally, the door broke open and the creature wriggled through just as she reached the nearest pillar and dug her nails into the oak. They held surprisingly well and she clawed her way upward.

The hybrid jumped up after her, its snapping jaws barely avoiding her legs as she pulled herself over the railing and landed on her shoulder. The Glock skidded away upon impact but she caught it before it could slide off the balcony. Groaning, she stood up, rubbing her arm. The monster was starting to climb the pillar, its eyes locked onto her with murderous intent.

Thinking quickly, Sydney aimed the gun down and fired. The bullet embedded itself in one of the creature's forearms and it fell back to the ground with a yelp. She watched as it angrily got up and limped back over, but couldn't do more than leap and scratch at the pillar with its injury.

Relieved, she turned and stumbled inside. She was back in the east guest room hallway. No one was in sight. She didn't remember which room Chang had been in, but she knew where Andy would be. Coming out onto the landing, she saw Graves's headless and half-eaten corpse. Blood and entrails were strewn about everywhere. She shivered.

The shape of the hybrid did not reappear through the shattered remnants of the front double doors, but it could be back at any moment. She was about to head down the west corridor to Andy's room when she heard a door opening behind her and whipped around, startled.

It was Andy. A look of surprise spread across his face. "Jesus, Sydney? Get in."

She slipped through the door and he swiftly closed and locked it. Chang walked over from farther into the room.

"What the hell did they do to you?" Andy said.

"The pills they gave me – it was lentiviral gene therapy carrying leopard DNA."

"The pills they gave all of us?" he asked.

She shook her head. "Just me and Brandon."

"Where is he?"

She gulped. "Dead, I think. They gave a different strain to him and it didn't go as well as they'd planned. He'd gone completely animalistic."

"How'd you get out of there?" Chang asked.

"It's complicated. Can you fly the plane?"

Chang nodded, but Sydney sensed unease in the room; both of them were clearly disturbed by her appearance. There was a mirror on the other side of the room, but she didn't want to look at it.

"There's still one of the hybrids out there," she said. "We'll never make it on foot."

"Then we drive," Chang said. "The SUV keys are all in the garage."

"We have to go past the front doors to get there, though," Sydney said. "It broke them open trying to get to me."

Chang eyed her pistol. "Can I have the gun?"

"Sure," Sydney said, handing her the Glock. *Does she not trust me with it?*

"I'll go first," Chang whispered, moving past her and carefully creaking the door open ever so slightly. Then she pushed the opening wider and walked forward, out of view. Sydney and Andy followed.

The lodge was quiet as they came out onto the landing. She tried not to look at Graves's remains as Chang led them down the stairs, the barrel of the Glock always focused on the ruined entrance.

Sydney kept watch behind them as they continued down the corridor to the right. Chang checked the corner to the staff quarters, but it was clear. They finally made it into the garage and hurriedly shut the door behind them.

Andy sighed with relief. "Let's get the hell out of here."

The space for the first Rover was empty, but the other four were plugged in and lined up in their usual formation. Sydney snatched the keys for the nearest one off the rack. "This one," she pointed, walking towards the car.

Andy went around back and unplugged it while Chang climbed into the driver's seat; both Sydney and Andy climbed into the back. The garage door retracted with the press of the button and the Land Rover flew out of the garage.

Chang abruptly braked and threw the wheel to the right,

swerving the vehicle around. She drove around the side of the garage and sped across the back field towards the paved trail.

"Any sign of that thing?" she said, her eyes darting to her passengers in the mirror.

"No," Andy said, looking out the back window.

"Good," Chang noted. "We should be there in no time."

Just as she began turning onto the walkway, Sydney heard a distant gunshot ring out and the front right tire blew. The Land Rover swerved and Chang struggled to regain control, roughly jerking the wheel in the opposite direction. But as the car swung back around and veered off the path, she was unable to turn it back again.

The SUV plowed into a nearby tree, and Sydney felt restrained by her safety belt as she heard the front of the car folding in on itself. Then she was thrown back into her seat, dazed. For about a minute, she blacked out.

Everything was blurry when she came to her senses. Her neck hurt from the whiplash, but other than that she seemed okay. Andy was starting to come to beside her.

"Are you alright?" he asked.

Before she could answer, a figure appeared in the window next to him. She opened her mouth to warn him, but it was too late. The butt of a rifle broke through the glass and hit him on the back of the head. He slumped over, suspended by the strap.

The figure was already gone, a shape moving around the back window. She fumbled with her seatbelt's holster as they drew nearer, almost to her side. She managed to press the release and the metal hook clicked free. Then the door flung open, a hand roughly grabbing her shoulder and hauling her out of the car. She fell to the ground, rolling onto her back on the grass.

A man stood over her, dressed in safari gear. There was a deep cut on his cheek and his hair, normally combed neatly, was an unkempt mess. Parts of him were covered in dirt and a weathered hunting rifle hung in his hands. His blue eyes glared down at her but his face wasn't contorted in anger; his expression was calm and measured.

"You have two minutes' head-start, so get running," Sans said, glancing at his hefty Pathfinder watch. "Then the game begins."

HUNTED

The pain of the crash evaporated as adrenaline flooded her body. She was on her feet in an instant, scrambling up the hillside path. She was surprised by how fast she could run and soon found herself at the edge of the tarmac. This was only one end of the airstrip, and the rest of it extended barely two thousand feet to the east. There were trees everywhere but the clearing seemed to be man-made.

At this end of the runway was a hangar where the Cessna sat waiting. The communications tower was located about two hundred feet to her left. Across from her was more forest and lush green overgrowth. Without thinking, she ran across the asphalt and smashed through a bush, stumbling deeper into the woodland.

The forest wasn't dense; rather it was an archipelago of various tree clusters that sometimes blurred together. Numerous open spaces and small clearings abounded with patches of the region's signature beige-green grass.

Had it been two minutes yet? She knew Sans would be at the top of the plateau in a flash.

She hid behind a tree for a moment to catch her breath. *Think*, she told herself. Hunting wasn't a sport of mindless shooting, it was a game of strategy where the stakes were life and death. First, Sans would try to guess where she had gone. Around here, there weren't many options. He might check the hangar, but he'd know she'd be smarter than that. Even if she hid in the plane, there would be no escape when he opened the door.

She began running again, thoughts swimming through her mind. He would guess that she had run off into the forest, and that's when he would have to resort to tracking techniques: her footprints, signs of disturbed flora, etc. She didn't know how far back the plateau extended, but she recalled there being more savanna on the other side during the flight in. The grass wouldn't help her; Sans would leisurely pick her off from the treeline.

The trees. He'd given her these attributes to make it more of a challenge. *I'll fucking give him one*, she decided.

She tilted her head back as she ran, her eyes darting between the treetops to see which would have the most foliage. One to her right looked good enough.

Without wasting a second, she leapt up and dug her claws into the bark, climbing onto the nearest sturdy branch. Then she grabbed a higher one and hauled herself up, hooking the talons of her feet into the main trunk to give her a better foothold. She made it to the highest branch that could support her and clung to it for dear life.

Through the leaves she could see that she had a much better view from here, roughly twenty feet up. Nothing moved below her that she could see. A gentle breeze drifted through the treetops, but it did little to calm her. Her heart was thumping rapidly and her stomach was twisting in on itself with hunger; she hoped the grumbling wasn't audible at ground level.

Carefully, she tried to turn around enough to see the other direction, which was mostly obscured by leaves. Still, it seemed as if the plateau extended another hundred feet or so, then began to slope down gentler than it did on the northern side toward the open savanna.

A few more minutes passed; Sans failed to appear. Sydney wasn't sure if that was a good sign or a bad sign. Years of research and a very expensive facility had just been destroyed, plus all his staff were dead. It would be hard to find new people that unquestioningly devoted and loyal to him. It was possible in his rage-induced state that he wasn't thinking clearly, and if he wasn't at the top of his game she could use that to her advantage.

She needed a plan. There was only one of him and one of her. Could she take him? The best bet would be if he unknowingly walked right beneath her and she could drop down, slicing her talons through him with gravity's aid.

Then it hit her: the claw marks. He'd obviously be able to see that she'd climbed this tree from the scratches in the bark. Then all he'd have to do was walk under her, aim up, and it'd be a turkey shoot.

She was toast. There was no other option: she would have to climb down.

Carefully, so as to not make too much noise, she began to lower her legs to the next branch. She dug her toes into the wood for support, then brought the rest of her body down in a crouch. After the next branch, she'd be able to jump.

A gun went off in the distance and part of the bark next to her exploded into splinters. She brought up her arm to shield her eyes in the nick of time, but lost her balance and toppled out of the tree.

It was nearly ten feet to the ground from there and

somehow she managed to land on her hands and knees. Still, the impact hurt like hell and she collapsed to the ground. As she tried to pull herself back up, it felt like something was broken, or least very badly bruised.

She hovered there dazed, battered, and hungry, then gave up and collapsed into the dirt.

Fifty feet away, Sans lowered the rifle. For a moment, it'd looked like she was trying to get back up, but now it was clear to him that she was down. As he began to walk towards her, he shook his head.

After single-handedly bringing about the destruction of the labs and the emitter field, costing him millions of dollars and the lives of fifteen people – sixteen if Brandon was counted, but he'd already been dead in Sans's eyes anyway – he'd expected the leopard girl to be the most thrilling prey of his life. And yet he'd still bagged her ten minutes in with a well-placed shot to a mobile shape amongst some leaves.

He could make out the scratched bark from here with ease, and once he thought he'd seen something moving, instinct took over. Raising, aiming, and squeezing the trigger had almost been involuntary, subconscious reflexes.

It was only just after seven o'clock and it'd already been one hell of a day.

He finally approached the form of the creature where she lay. Her body was completely unmoving. There was no doubt about it, she was dead. She lay on her stomach so he guessed the entry wound must've been on the chest or abdomen.

Sans bent down and grabbed her shoulder, feeling the course fur beneath his fingers as he turned the body over for a look–

And the thing suddenly sprung to life, digging her claws

into his left side and tearing down to his hip. Sans screamed at the top of his lungs, his right arm swinging the butt of the rifle around to knock her off of him. It worked and he tumbled to the ground, clutching his horrific wound. Blood gushed all over his fingers.

Swiftly, he pulled out his hunting knife as she lunged for him again, and he just managed to bring it up as she swiped her crimson-covered claws downward. The blade went straight through her palm and out the other side. She howled and reeled back, taking the knife with her.

He watched as she furiously began to pull it out of her hand and he grasped for his rifle beside him. He was on his feet in a flash and swung the butt of the gun again just as she got the blade free. Upon impact, the knife tumbled away and she fell to the ground.

But she was quick, this prey, already back on her feet as he fired. She narrowly dodged the bullet and jumped towards him. He turned his back to her and she latched onto him from behind, digging her feet's claws into his hamstrings, her fingernails cutting into his arms.

He screamed again and forced himself backwards, slamming her into the tree. She clenched harder, her mouth closing atop his left shoulder. The next thing he knew, she'd taken a chunk of flesh out and blood was running down his shirt.

Angrily, he slammed back again, this time harder. It seemed to have more of an effect and he did it a third time. She finally slipped off as he fell forward. In an instant, he found his gun and swirled around to aim for her–

Except she was gone.

Slowly and on edge, he got to his feet. *Where the fuck did she go?* he thought. She still had to be nearby.

But all around him was quiet save for the morning caw of birds. He aimed the barrel up into the tree; he swept it all around him.

Gone.

Clearly, he had scared her off for a moment. His hunting knife was still lying on the ground, which meant she hadn't taken it. He took a moment to examine himself: his khaki fatigues were shredded and bloodied. The gash on his side was the worst; she'd gotten him deep there and the blood was still flowing freely.

He started to feel dizzy, then shook it off. *You haven't lost nearly enough yet*, he told himself. The average man of his weight had over one and a half gallons of vascular fluid. He just needed to get back to the lodge and patch himself up. It was bright enough that all the other hybrids should've retreated by now.

Doing one final check to make sure the leopard girl wasn't around, he began to stumble back the way he came with the rifle at his side. One hand was pressed tightly against as much of the four-clawed tear as he could, but it extended from his lower ribs to his hip bone. Blood was trickling down his leg. He tried not think about that, or the sting, or anything other than keeping alert.

There was a noise from the bushes off to his left, and Sans spun and fired. Nothing. The chamber was empty and he quickly worked to reload it, his eyes glancing up and around to make sure nothing lurked in his peripheral.

Then he continued. Something was watching him, he was sure of it. He could feel its predatory gaze like a sixth sense. He contemplated running, but his side hurt too much for that to be effective. How far was the bloody airstrip? There had to be a first-aid kit in the hanger, and certainly in the plane if nowhere else.

Leaves rustled above and he brought the barrel upward, firing through the branches. Nothing fell save for his hopes as he continued backing through the underbrush. Sans came out into another small clearing area, where at least he knew he'd be safe from her pouncing out of a tree.

He was starting to feel woozy; his left leg was caked in blood that ran all the way to his white socks, staining them a dark red. Sans was too busy staring back the way he came to care. He knew she was out there. He could feel her watching him. And yet he had no idea where the hell she was.

Gradually, he kept retreating slowly back towards the runway. He knew it had to be close. His gun was at the ready and he felt his skin cool slightly as he entered the shade of a tree behind him. All was quiet before him, but he had a better view of his surroundings from here.

Then, procedurally, he turned around and checked his six. Nothing moved.

There was a *crack* in a branch above him.

Sans brought the rifle up but she was already falling towards him, teeth bared and claws outstretched. She didn't land on his back, but came down behind him as her talons raked along his spine.

Immediately, the rifle slipped from his grasp and he tumbled into the tall grass, his body racked in too much pain to move. He lay just beyond the threshold of the shade at the edge of the clearing, and watched as she swiftly got out of her catlike crouch and prepared to pounce.

There was nothing human-like about her mannerisms, he thought to himself almost with a smile. That, at least, had gone perfectly. For a moment, he took her in, the dimmed light around her highlighting the soft glow of the yellow eyes and the blood dripping from her chin – his blood. Her open mouth revealed terrifyingly pointed teeth.

For a brief instant, Sans felt a sensation he'd almost forgotten – the frosty chill of fear.

All he managed was a brief, sharp cry. Then the leopard girl landed on top of him, her claws digging through his flesh for purchase as she plunged her teeth into his throat.

A small flock of birds scattered towards the morning sun above the treetops.

For Billy Sans, one of eastern Africa's most experienced big-game hunters, the last safari was over.

TAKEOFF

Chang slowly blinked into consciousness. There was blood in her eyes and she had a moment of panic, then realized it was just from a cut on her forehead. She was leaning against the deployed steering wheel airbag and didn't appear to be badly injured. The left rear door was open and Sydney was gone; Andy was unconscious and held relatively upright by his seatbelt. She saw that his window had been smashed.

Sans.

Undoing her seatbelt, she felt around on the floor in front of the passenger seat for the Glock. She found it under the glove box, then opened the door and stumbled outside. The temperature was rising with the sun as she made her way around the back of the car and threw Andy's door open.

"Are you alright?" she said, gently shaking his shoulder.

Slowly, he came around. "What happened?" he asked, putting his hand to the back of his head. His fingers came away with blood; he'd clearly been hit.

"We're getting out of here." She helped him undo his seatbelt and slung his arm over her shoulder. Then they walked back onto the paved trail and continued up the hill.

"Where's Sydney?" he mumbled.

"We're going to find her," Chang said. Her eyes were alert for any movement in the trees on either side of them, just in case there were still any hybrids afoot.

Finally, they reached the top of the hill and found themselves at the edge of the plateau's airstrip. She looked towards the hangar. "There's gotta be a first aid kit in there," she said.

Andy shook his head. "I'll be fine. We need to find Sydney."

Chang looked around, but there was no sign of her or Sans. She assumed he'd chased Sydney off into the woods somewhere and figured it would be best to wait until one of them came back. If it was Sans who emerged from the trees battered and bruised, she was prepared to put a bullet in him immediately. He'd become a dog that needed to be put down.

That's one way to oust a CEO, she thought. *No one on the board will ever fuck with me again.* The thought almost brought a smile to her face, but she wouldn't allow herself one until they were flying out of here.

"Let's just get the plane ready first and–"

"We *have* to find her," he said, moving off her shoulder. His motivation seemed to heal him, at least for the time being. "Please."

"We have no clue where they went."

"There's only one way they could have gone." Andy pointed to the trees ahead. "That way."

Chang sighed. "Then let's go."

They walked across the tarmac and into the patchy woodland. She swatted mosquitos away from her face and kept her finger on the Glock's trigger. There was no sign of wildlife save for a few birds singing high on a branch somewhere. They continued hiking for awhile and Chang was tempted to say they should head back when Andy suddenly stopped. She looked too.

About twenty feet ahead, at the edge of a tiny clearing, lay the bloodied body of a man. Cautiously, the two of them stepped closer for a better look and saw that it was Sans, horrifically mauled and eviscerated. It wasn't a pretty sight. Chang felt bile rising in her throat and turned away.

"Are there still hybrids around here?" she said.

"It should be too bright for them."

She began moving. "We better get back to the–"

She froze. Andy followed her line of sight and stopped too. They both knew what had killed Sans.

An animalistic figure was standing about thirty feet away. There was blood all over her mouth and claws, but she looked more ashamed than territorial as she froze before them.

"Sydney?" he called.

She took a step towards them when Chang suddenly raised the Glock and fired.

It missed, but Sydney turned and scrambled away into the underbrush.

"What the hell are you doing?" Andy snapped.

"Didn't you see? She's gone completely feral!"

"She killed him in self-defense!"

"She ripped him to fucking shreds and ate him! She's too dangerous to be brought back! We have to go. Now!" She took off in a sprint back towards the airfield.

"Wait!" he cried after her, but it was no use. There was no choice but to follow her.

By the time he reached the hangar, he found her opening the rear door of the plane and ascending the stairs. "Come on!" she called.

Frantically, he looked back at the forest. Sydney was nowhere in sight. "Shit," he muttered, and ran for the aircraft. After he had closed the door behind him and joined her in the cockpit, Chang turned to him as she began the pre-flight check.

"It's not her fault," she said. "It was *his*."

"We don't have to leave her here. We could sedate her, bring her back and try to fix her."

Chang shook her head. "The research is gone. I'm sorry, I didn't want to do this but she's beyond help. You have to understand that she's not a person anymore."

The next thing he knew, they were starting down the landing strip. Andy felt an uneasy serenity watching the trees whip by as the aircraft sped down the tarmac. Then the ground fell away.

From the top of a tree on the northern side of the plateau, Sydney watched as the plane banked to the left and flew off towards the distant reaches of the savanna.

She continued watching as it dwindled into a little speck in the sky. By the time it vanished, there were tears rolling down her cheeks.

RETURN

The sun was getting low beyond the Potomac view of the boardroom's panoramic windows, bathing the place in an evening glow. Chang and a suited man sat on the other side of the table, files and stacks of papers littering the mahogany between them.

He had introduced himself as Derek Marder, the COO. He was a lean corporate type with silvery gray hair but not a wrinkle on his face. "The team made a final sweep of the facility yesterday. Sans and his personal staff are all confirmed dead, as well as seven of the hybrid creatures you and Ms. Chang described. That leaves five unaccounted for."

"Did they get off the reserve?" Andy asked.

"Unfortunately, it appears so," Chang said. "An unusual animal attack was reported in Serengeti National Park two days ago. An entire group of zebras was found brutally slaughtered, but each was only partially eaten. We've hired Solomon Akeda, a respected zoologist who was at the scene, to spearhead the search."

"Why would the animals do that?" Marder asked.

"Probably establishing territory," Andy suggested. "They're expanding, seeing where on the food chain they fit in the new ecosystem."

"Yes," Marder said, shuffling papers. "Which is very, very bad. Akeda's team is trying to track them down, but it's going to be hard to keep this quiet. Not to mention the millions of dollars in research we've lost and telling the truth to the families about how their children *really* died. It's not a good time for anyone right now."

"The legal department has advised me against speaking about the nature of the settlements we're preparing," Chang said. "But just between us, Andy, I doubt SansCorp will be able to recover from this."

He silently gazed out at the river, unsure of what to say.

"Your family is still picking you up tomorrow?" Marder asked.

"Yes," Andy said. "When I called them, they were quite surprised to learn I was still alive."

"I'm sure they'll be glad to see you in person. And the hotel has been fine?"

"Perfectly fine, sir."

"It's the least we could do." Chang smiled, then her mood grew somber. "I'm really sorry this all happened."

"It's none of our faults," he said, watching his fingers tap on the wood. Then he looked up. "Was there any sign of Sydney?"

Marder shook his head. "They've combed the entire reserve. No trace of her."

Andy silently nodded.

"Okay, that's it," Chang said. "We'll keep you updated."

Andy got up, pushed in the chair, and exited back into the hallway. He took the elevator down, walked past the reception with the large, sleek SansCorp logo emblazoned on the wall, and came outside into a gentle summer evening's breeze.

There was something he needed to do, but he checked his watch. It was almost ten to seven. They were usually closed by now. Unless... He pulled out his phone and quickly Googled something. Sure enough, it was open today until 7:30 due to Extended Summer Hours. He could make it if he got there quickly.

Andy requested an Uber, which arrived two minutes later. The drive from Bethesda to downtown D.C. took roughly half an hour, but he finally stepped out onto the sidewalk and glanced towards the Washington Monument down the Mall. The Capitol Building wasn't far behind him. But he didn't even pause to take in those sights, running up the stairs to the building's grand entrance.

At the security check inside, the guard told him: "We're closing in less than ten minutes."

"That's fine," he said. "There's just one thing I need to see."

He briskly walked to the left of the main rotunda with its enormous elephant display and continued into the Hall of Mammals. Crowds of people were gently drifting out as he made his way to the Africa exhibit. It was just as he'd seen it two weeks before, but it felt different now. Empty almost, and not because he was one of the few people still here. As he walked up the ramp leading deeper into the hall, he paused to look up at the leopard, staring off into an imagined savanna with its kill slung over the branch beside it.

Andy tried to imagine her up in a tree like that one, looking out on her new domain with the pride of an apex predator–free to roam the land on an endless safari, unrestricted by society's constraints just as she'd always dreamed. Regardless of wherever she was or what became of her, he knew one thing was certain. She would always be human to him.

ACKNOWLEDGEMENTS

I'd like to thank the people who have helped me with the preparation of this novel: my Dreyfoos creative writing teachers Brittany Rigdon, Angela Weber, Brittany Ackerman, and Donovan Ortega, and my biology teacher Stephen Anand. I'd also like to thank 'Uncle' Edward Seagram and 'Uncle' Phillip Benson for their insights on hunting, and Jane Snook for her photographs and tales of Africa that served as inspiration for the setting. And lastly, to my mother and editor Barbara for providing invaluable support and insight throughout the writing process.